THE SWEET ROAD HOME

<u>THE SWEET ROAD HOME</u>

JOIN THE JACKI KELLY NEWSLETTER
at
Jackikelly.com

Get a free book and stay tuned to new releases, appearance and events and prizes. She's always giving something away.

Prologue

June 1999

Simeon Harper squinted against the hot summer sun to make out Asa Conroy in the distance. Unsure if he loved or hated her, he couldn't deny she was the prettiest girl at Northwestern High School. Her creamy skin bore a hint of chocolate and her lush, dark curls captured his attention every time she came within fifty feet.

Across the span of the parking lot, he watched her place a disc into her CD player. This was his favorite way to view Asa. From a distance, he didn't have to worry about his words getting twisted in his mouth and stumbling all over himself like a fool. Maybe from here he looked like the coolest person in their class, instead of the son of the town drunk.

"Come on, boy, we gotta get home." Brian slapped him on the back.

"Yeah, I'm coming, bro. Do you think we can go to the Conroy block party this weekend? We never go." Simeon didn't take his eyes off Asa. She bobbed her head to the music playing in her ear.

"Hell no, we ain't going. You know we can't."

Simeon sensed his brother's annoyance. "Look at you. Your pants are too small, they're raggedy, and if your hair grows another inch you'll look like Jimi Hendrix. Those Conroys don't want nothing to do with people like us. Why are you always asking about going over there? We haven't been and we won't start now. We belong over here and they belong over there." He drew an imaginary line with his foot. "Now come on, if we're late it just gives Dad another reason to get angry." Brian walked away without glancing back.

Before Simeon could catch up to his brother, Asa waved and started in his direction. He swallowed hard against the lump in his throat. Maybe this time his words wouldn't get stuck. Her carefree gait matched her demeanor. Her eyes sparkled like the glass shards that littered the park at his housing project. Every time he saw her, she wore a smile. Life treated the Conroys well; the Harpers always drew leftovers. Her shiny red CD player mocked him, emphasizing everything he wasn't.

She removed the plugs from her ears. He froze.

§ § §

In grade school Simeon had pulled her ponytail, stolen her lunch, and peered under her dress. Now Asa wanted him to venture under her dress. Despite her mother's abstinence sermon, he would have gotten to second base. Instead, he acted like she didn't exist.

The way he buried his nose in the books, her grandmother would have called him an old soul. His playfulness had vanished. Now he was all grunts or groans.

Today determination drove her to get his attention. Something about his pecan brown, Shemar Moore good looks, dimpled cheek, and wide smile yanked her across the parking lot toward him. This was her last opportunity before going to college to get what she wanted. Him.

"Hey, Simeon, are you coming to our party on Saturday?"

Instead of answering, his eyes narrowed as they raked over her. Why did he always look so angry?

"Aren't you coming?" she asked again.

His nostrils flared.

Asa recoiled. Her heart skidded against her ribs.

Before she could flinch, he smacked her CD player out of her hand. It whacked the concrete so hard several pieces of shiny red plastic flew across the pavement.

Chapter One

This is crazy. Could life get back to normal with a simple change of addresses? Asa Conroy flung her sunglasses across the dashboard and glared at the run-down house in front of her. She flexed her fingers and rolled her shoulders to release the tension from the twelve-hour drive from Atlanta. Her late model Mercedes sputtered, punctuating her arrival in Bristol, Delaware.

Her cell phone vibrated against the passenger seat. Eric, her ex-husband, had started calling ten hours ago. She refused to answer the annoying interruption. His ranting grew more persistent when she refused to entertain his apology.

She surveyed her grandparents' house through the bug-splattered windshield. It didn't look inviting. A faded and tattered shutter hung at an ugly angle, the torn screen door blew in the afternoon breeze, and weeds threatened to overtake the yard. But this was home, where she grew up, the only place where she could put her life back together.

Her adorable, dizzy sister, Dakota, had promised to stop by and remove the dust covers from the furniture, turn on the utilities, and stock the refrigerator. From the deserted look of the large colonial, she hadn't done much. Asa wished she had followed her instincts and hired a cleaning crew to get the house ready. Her schedule for the next few weeks didn't allow time for domestic activity.

Instead of unpacking everything stuffed in the trunk, she shoved her cell phone into her purse, grabbed her overnight bag, and trudged up the rickety wooden stairs. Everything she needed tonight fit into one of these two bags. She was too exhausted to unload anything else.

The stairs creaked, piercing the quiet surroundings. She stuck her key in the lock and turned the knob. The door didn't budge. She dropped her bags at her feet, sized up the task, then threw her hip against the door. It swung open with such force that she stumbled into the narrow hallway.

She groped for and found the wall switch. Dim light illuminated the front hall and threw a band of gloss across the scarred wooden floors.

Sheets covered everything. It didn't surprise her that Dakota had forgotten to keep her promise. The interior of the house looked almost as bad as the exterior. A musty smell permeated the air and a layer of dust covered everything. Despite the odor, her chest puffed with happiness. Now she could start over. Joyful anticipation made her knees tremble.

Her cell phone rang, again. She fished it out of her purse. Before accepting the call, she checked to make sure it wasn't her stalker ex-husband. Her sister, Melissa's number appeared in the display.

"Hey, what's up?"

"Why haven't you been accepting my calls? I've been trying to reach you for two days." Melissa's shrill voice pierced the silence in the room.

"Eric kept bugging me, so I stopped picking up."

"Well, while you're trying to dodge your crazy ex did it dawn on you that you might miss some other important calls? That's so much like you, Asa, always taking the passive-aggressive route. I thought you would have some backbone by now."

"Look, Melissa, I wanted to concentrate on the road, I didn't need the distraction." Asa plopped down on the sofa and massaged her temple. "What's so important?

"Where are you?"

"In Bristol. I just got here. I haven't been in the house ten minutes yet."

"What took you so long? I thought you were getting in yesterday."

"I had car trouble, and stopped in D.C. to look at a boutique on Connecticut Avenue. They're featuring my spring line." Asa fingered a curl on her forehead.

"Did Dakota tell you about the house?"

"Tell me what? That it needs a thorough cleaning? You know how forgetful she is. She didn't even open the house like we agreed. The electricity is on but I'll bet there isn't any food in the fridge." She fell back against the sofa. A plume of dust rose around her. "The house looks abandoned. Why isn't Dakota keeping the place up?"

"Did she tell you about the house?" Melissa's voice was tense.

Panic crawled up her spine. "Tell me what, Melissa? Why can't you tell me?" She couldn't suppress the edge in her voice.

"Look, I don't know how long you plan to stay, but the house is being torn down in a few months to make way for a strip mall. I signed a preliminary agreement with

Simeon's company a few weeks ago. Once they've completed the due diligence, we'll sign the final contract."

Asa squeezed her eyes against the sharp pain churning in her gut. "What did you say?" Her hands trembled. Her heart thundered against her ribs. "Simeon Harper?"

"Yes, it's his company's project. It shouldn't be a problem, you usually only stay a few days anyway."

"Did you say the house is being torn down?" Asa shouted into the mouthpiece.

"Yes, calm down. What is your problem?"

"It shouldn't cause a problem for who, Melissa? For you? Why am I just now hearing about this? "

"I know Mim and Pepa left the house to the three of us. I thought this is what you and Dakota wanted. This offer came along...I took it."

Asa groaned. She had a vague recollection of conversations about selling the property, after her grandmother's death, but between grieving for her grandmother and bemoaning her failing marriage, she hadn't paid much attention.

"The house is a money pit, we need to run while we can," Melissa continued.

"I'm willing to buy you and Dakota out. I want the house." Asa rubbed her forehead.

"Well," Melissa hesitated. "They're looking to see what, if any, liens exist on the houses, checking surveys, and zoning permits; stuff like that. If everything checks out then we move forward to final contract."

Tension crept back into Asa's shoulders. She slumped against the couch. Her sisters didn't know this trip to Bristol wasn't a visit—it was permanent. She planned to live happily in the house where she grew up. Why was it talking to her sisters more difficult than talking with a strangers? Hearing their judgment-laced speeches about running away again would make her scream. That was why she didn't bother telling them her plans.

"Are you there, Asa?" The exasperation in Melissa's voice clawed her skin like a cat.

"Yeah, I'm here. Look Melissa, I didn't mention my plans to you or Dakota, but I'm moving back permanently. This summer, I need to finish my designs and renovate a studio. I had no idea you were even considering selling the house."

Melissa snorted. "Well, Asa, I didn't know you'd ever think about moving back to Bristol to live. Why don't you come out to California and stay with me and Darius. We have plenty of room."

She and Melissa got along about as well as Tom and Jerry. After constantly matching wits with Eric she didn't intend to repeat the bitterness again with Melissa. She wanted tranquility. "I'm staying here."

"Are you running from something?"
Asa rolled her eyes toward the ceiling. "No. I just wanted to
come home." Asa gulped for air.

"Well— that's up to you. I have a letter here that says there's a meeting tonight at the high school." She heard Melissa shuffle through some papers. "The developer will review the plans and answer the residents' questions. If you want to know more about the project then you should go."

"Thanks a lot." Asa disconnected the call and fell back against the sofa. Her mind went blank as she concentrated on the crack in the ceiling that stretched from one end of the room to the next. She closed her eyes and tried to recall if it had been there the last time she came home. No, she didn't think so.

Her fists clenched at her sides. How did bad luck find her so fast? "I should get in the car and keep driving until it runs out of gas?"

Melissa climbed out of the womb knowing what she wanted and how to get it. Asa was still looking. And by her sister's account, she didn't have a clue. She curled up on the sofa until her heartbeat returned to normal. Laying there she could almost feel her grandmother's soothing fingers stroking her back. This was home. This was the only place where she felt loved. Now Simeon wanted to take her security away.

The sound of scratching broke into her thoughts. For a moment she tried to label the sound. Instead of investigating she bolted upright, punched Dakota's number into her cell phone and pounced on her sister as soon as she answered. "Dakota, did you know about the house?"

"Hey, where are you?" Dakota was stalling, Asa could tell by her slow speech.

"Did you know?" Asa asked again between clenched teeth.

"I meant to tell you about that. I forgot. Every time I picked up the phone something happened in the store." Dakota paused. "You're not upset, are you?"

"Hell yes, I'm upset. How could both you and Melissa fail to tell me about this?"

"Well, you were dealing with Eric and working on your designs for Fashion Week, so..."

"Melissa mentioned a meeting, are you going?"

"No, I wasn't."

Asa jumped up and another cloud of dust followed her. "I'll pick you up in five minutes. I need to find out what's going on."

Asa pushed her way to the front of the crowded school auditorium. Her stomach twisted in a tight knot. The meeting was beginning and she wanted a seat in the first row. The crumpled meeting agenda left ink stains in her sweaty palm. She didn't need a piece of paper to remind her what she wanted to do.

How could Simeon Harper still turn her life upside down after ten years? Most of the time in high school he ignored her, barely acknowledging her existence. Now his strip mall threatened the one place she felt happy and safe.

Her curiosity compelled her to hurry to the empty seats in the front of the room. So privately agog about Simeon's intentions that she had to remember to greet her gathering neighbors. When she saw Simeon eyes then she would know whether his project should be taken as a personal affront against her and her family or not. Eyes never change. Emotions always showed in the eyes.

Asa took the seat next to her sister. The deafening chatter in the room made it hard to hear.

"Look at all these people. I hope they're here to support the block and not the strip mall." Asa glanced around the room hoping to find support.

Dakota nodded, her huge afro swayed back and forth. Asa leaned close to her sister and whispered. "I can't believe I had a crush on Simeon in high school. I thought he was the most handsome boy in our class."

"You can see for yourself, he's still hot." Dakota pointed to a group of men standing in the far corner.

There he was. Asa's eyes followed the length of his frame. For a brief moment, the room stood still. No one seemed to move or utter a word. The only thing she heard was the ear-splitting sound of her blood rushing in her ears. She swallowed. Her eyes lingered on his chiseled jaw and warm brown complexion. She exhaled slowly through her nose while forcing her body to remain calm.

Some people don't change and he didn't disappoint her. He looked even better than she remembered. His thick lashes fluttered over his dark brown eyes and the smile he reserved for everyone else spread across his strikingly handsome face. He stood taller and leaner than the other men gathered near the podium. In a room of NBA players, maybe he wouldn't stand out, but in this crowd of Golden Leaf residents and a few suited gentlemen he was easy to spot. His custom fitted suit was a huge contrast to the rag-tag clothes he wore to school. That handsome hunk talking to the group of men seemed self-assured and confident, not the brooding teenager she once fixated on. Would he remember the last time they saw each other? She doubted it. He probably had no idea how hurt she was that day in the parking lot.

"Aren't you going to say something to him?" Dakota nudged her.

"Let's wait until after the meeting. Maybe he has nothing to do with the project. I don't want to look foolish."

"Oh, he's the one all right. He's not the Simeon Harper you remember. These days, his name is stamped on almost every building project in the city." Dakota raised an eyebrow. "Nearly every woman in town flirts with him at some point. Since you had a crush on him, why don't you go on a date with Mr. Perfect? I think you two would make a good couple."

"When hell freezes over. The man is trying to tear down the house. If he has his way I could be homeless in months."

"Don't get so dramatic," Dakota sighed. "You know what I mean. Besides, even though my divorce is final, the last thing I want is to date anyone. I'm taking a hiatus from men until the studio is established and the fashion show is over."

"It's time to get back out there. You know Mim used to say, fall off a horse and get right back on."

"No thanks. I don't care for horses. First the house, then my studio and then the fashion show. That's my new mantra." Asa crossed her arms over her chest. Her heart was safely tucked away and she didn't intend to expose her emotions for another sacrificial offering.

The corners of her lips turned up. She leaned against her sister. "But if I ever change my mind, he's definitely the one I'd want between my sheets."

Dakota gave her a playful nudge.

Asa sat back. Thoughts of her ill-fated marriage and the resulting divorce decree buried in her trunk were enough to stave off men. When she returned home she might need to pull it out, just in case she felt compelled to rush into another relationship. Getting her design studio up and running needed her full attention.

"But—" Dakota started.

"Shh, the meeting is getting ready to start," Asa patted her sisters arm and leaned forward in her seat.

His confident swagger made her tingle. Simeon strolled across the stage to stand behind the podium. He cleared his throat and adjusted his papers. She squeezed the agenda tighter and concentrated on what he had to say. Understanding what he planned to do with her grandparent's house was the only thing that mattered.

As the lights dimmed he pointed to a detailed presentation. Several pictures of a sprawling planned community flashed on the screen. A community center with basketball courts, an indoor pool, game rooms, computer center, and a commercial- sized kitchen had several people cheering. One slide depicted cottage style housing for senior and disabled citizens. His presentation of the colorful strip mall, with red awnings, slated for the Golden Leaf area drew jeers from the back of room. The muscles in her back knotted. A dry cleaner occupied the space where her home now stood.

Asa used her hand to smooth the agenda against her thigh.

Swallowing hard as she tried to make sense of his project, she scribbled dates and locations into the margins of the wrinkled paper. The image of Simeon's broad shoulders and muscular build made it hard to concentrate. After all these years, his voice still sent ripples down her spine. But saving the house was too important to focus on anything else.

In the ten years since leaving, he'd grown taller and morphed into a charismatic man. With a boyish charm he never possessed in high school he strolled around the podium discussing the two projects' benefits. His deep voice filled the room as he commanded the auditorium.

Everyone's eyes focused on him. He rolled through the papers in front of him with ease. His long, lean fingers restacked the papers, banging them against the podium to indicate his presentation was finished.

"I'd like to thank all of you for coming out tonight. You can see the design for the community center or the mall on the website listed on the program. Also, if you have any questions please feel free to contact my office." He took a step away from the podium and flashed a smile directly at her.

"Hey, Mr. Big Shot," a man shouted from the back of the room. "Just where are we supposed to live now?"

Simeon stopped and faced the crowd. "Everyone is

being compensated handsomely for their homes. If you don't think your offer is commensurate with the value of your house, please contact my offices."

"You bet I will," the man huffed.

Asa watched the exchange with her mouth open. "I wonder if he'll have the same tone after talking to me?" she asked her sister.

The crowd rushed to their feet. Some moved for the back doors. Others elbowed through them pressing toward the front of the room. Asa stepped aside, gathering her thoughts. Forming a coherent sentence seemed impossible. This wasn't the place to discuss her issue. She needed a different approach. Getting him alone could work in her favor.

His infamous good looks and dimpled cheeks were familiar. But the way this man finessed the crowd, he could make them believe in Santa Claus. Even the angry gentleman seemed pacified now. The Simeon she remembered couldn't, or wouldn't do that.

Several women stood in the line to talk to Simeon. From the way they refreshed their lipstick and patted their stylish hairdos, Golden Leaf wasn't what drew them to the school tonight.

"How do I look?" Asa asked Dakota, suddenly feeling underdressed. Her jean shorts and lace tee seemed inappropriate now.

"You look fine. Why?" Dakota turned around to see what Asa was looking at. "Oh, well, you're not showing as much cleavage as that woman, but you look fine. This is a school, not a night club." Dakota pushed her forward. "Now go up there and ask your questions so we can get out of here. I saw him smile at you,"

"You need to stop. Girl, there are nearly a hundred people in this room. I think he smiled at all of us. He needs to smile at every homeowner that lives at Golden Leaf to make sure we agree with his project. But I'm not falling for his charm, smooth talk, or his plans. Why in the world would he want to tear down all those houses? We need another strip mall around here about as much as we need a basement full of rats."

"Oh boy," Dakota sighed. "There you go."

"You know I'm right. That neighborhood is great. The houses are historic. We had a great time growing up there. Remember the fantastic block parties we had every summer?"

"Not as fondly as you do, evidently."

"Our parents and grandparents would turn over in their graves if they knew that house could be torn down. We have to try to save our memories for them."

"I was there last week when I had the electricity turned on and I didn't get a warm, fuzzy feeling about the house. Instead it felt a little creepy to me." Dakota shivered.

Asa eyed her sister. "Well maybe you need to spend a little more time there. My first few minutes felt great, until Melissa called."

"And you think the feeling was because of the house? Maybe that warm feeling was because you were closer to people who love you or because you were closer to

Simeon. Everybody knew you had a crush on him. Maybe you still do," Dakota snickered.

Asa ignored her sister. "I'm going up there to talk to him."

"Just remember, be nice. It's like Mim always said, you can catch more flies with honey than vinegar."

"Mim had lots of sayings. Remember the one about be it ever so humble, there's no place like home? It seems you and Melissa forgot that one."

Dakota shrugged. "I'm just saying be nice. Don't lose your temper."

"Of course, I'll be nice. I'm going to present the facts...he can't ignore facts. Besides, since he has so much money, he can find another tract of land to build his mall."

Dakota's dubious look didn't go undetected. Asa shook her finger at her sister and made her way to the podium. She fell in line behind a woman that reeked of perfume and openly flirted with Simeon. She purred his name the way a woman does when trying to entice a man. Asa slapped her flip-flop against the cement floor while she waited for the ridiculous spectacle to end. The woman placed her hand on his shoulder, faking laughter at something he said. He shifted just enough to escape her touch. The elusive Simeon hadn't changed; the ice cube embedded in his heart remained intact.

Asa hadn't been this close to Simeon since that unfortunate day in the school parking lot. Excitement coursed through her veins. Maybe this time she could tease him like he teased her in school. Let him do a little panting while she cruised out of his life. It would serve him right.

Her planned speech evaporated on her tongue as she watched his luscious lips. He glanced over the woman's shoulder. His dark eyes drew Asa closer as warmth crawled up her spine and settled in her neck. She looked away until the woman finally ended her flirting and stepped aside.

In front of him she pushed her shoulders back and smiled. His aftershave smelled as good as he looked. The black flecks in his chocolate brown eyes made him look hunky and tempting. If she focused on those eyes, she would follow him anywhere, like Hansel and Gretel following crumbs through the forest. He cleared his throat and broke her trance.

"Simeon you might not remember me." She stuck out her hand and gave him a firm handshake. "We went to high school together. I'm Asa Suarez...um...Conroy." She scrambled for something more to say.

"Yes, I remember you. What can I do for you, Asa Suarez Conroy?"

"No, it's just Asa Conroy now. I've been divorced for two years; sometimes I still slip up." She pushed a handful of curls behind her ear. "Anyway, I'd like to talk with you about this project--the strip mall. My grandparent's house will be impacted by it."

"I see." He took a wider stance, clasped his hands and held her gaze. "You haven't changed much since high school." He flashed a smile.

He was capable of emotion; who knew? Her stomach

somersaulted. She wasn't supposed to feel this way. Anything she felt for him should have died years ago. Play it cool girl.

From the corner of her eye, she saw Dakota nod with encouragement. Her sister's support helped bolster Asa's courage. "Can we talk?"

"Sure what would you like to know that wasn't already covered in this meeting?"

"Well I don't know much, only what you've shared tonight." She wrung her hands.

"We've sent quarterly notices to keep everyone informed."

"I haven't been following the notices. I just got in town tonight."

"I can have my administrative assistant get copies for you." The curl of his lip was sexy and seductive.

"That won't be necessary. I'm sure my sister can fill me in. Can we meet tomorrow and talk in private?" A little time would allow her to formulate a plan and quell the rebellion building in her stomach.

"There are so many people waiting to talk with you tonight. I don't want to hold up the line."

He hesitated; his eyes ran the length of her legs. "We can do that." He pulled his phone from his breast pocket and used his thumb to maneuver the screen. "How about tomorrow, we can have lunch at my offices and I can go over the plans with you?"

"I wasn't thinking of something so formal."

"I'll keep it casual, it's not a problem." He crossed his arms over his broad chest. His platinum Rolex flashed under the fluorescent lighting. Dakota had tagged it right. He was wealthy. He reached for her hand again. This time holding it longer than necessary, but even a millisecond would have been long enough for a rush of heat to shoot up her arm. Before she could read anything into the gesture, another resident drew his attention.

Asa stumbled away to find her sister talking with a small group. What just happened? The look, his touch, was he flirting? She was the one that was supposed to be flirting. Did the lack of male companionship over the last two years have her confused?

After all these years, the last thing she should have cared about is what Simeon thought about her, but she did.

§ § §

Simeon stared after Asa as she walked away. She had to be joking. Not remember her? Unable to forget her, came closer to describing his feelings. He had seen her walk into the auditorium. For a moment, he thought it might have been a Conroy cousin, but when she smiled, there was no mistaking it was Asa. The hairs on his arms stood at attention. Only Asa Conroy could cause that kind of reaction.

He chatted with one of the residents of Golden Leaf, but he couldn't take his eyes off Asa. The way she sashayed across the room was pure heaven. The familiar sway of her hips reminded him why he liked her so much in school. If possible, she looked even better now. The skinny high school cheerleader had blossomed into a stunning woman. The glow of her smooth complexion, along with the loose unruly curls made a spectacular package. Could her skin feel as soft as it appeared? After all these years, thoughts of Asa still swarmed in his head. Without her even knowing, she still held his heart and always would. His current appetite for her exceeded his childish crush. Thankfully, age made him wiser and in control of his desires.

He ran the back of his hand across his brow to wipe away beads of sweat.

"Did you hear me?"

"I'm sorry," Simeon focused his attention on the resident standing in front of him. "Please repeat that for me."

"You're still looking at that pretty girl you were just talking to. I don't blame you." The man rubbed his hands together. "If I wasn't married, I just might give you a run for your money."

"It's a good thing I don't have to compete with you." Simeon joked with the older man. He watched as Asa found her sister. The Conroy family always stuck together. He wasn't surprised to see two of them at this meeting tonight. There were probably more Conroys gathering in the parking lot to support Asa's mission. The Harper family could take a lesson from them.

"What can I do for you tonight?" Simeon turned back to the gentleman.

"I just want to thank you. It's a good thing you're doing

for the neighborhood. We need a place to shop, without having to go across town.”

After shaking the resident's hand Simeon sought out Asa again. The beautiful Asa was still as gorgeous as ever. Now she was divorced and available. He smiled. Maybe the time was right.

The poor, timid boy from high school disappeared the day they buried his father. Simeon lifted his chin and peered over the crowd. The Harper family name now represented prosperity and wealth. His current projects alone would net his company millions.

He sighed. Asa wanted to talk to him about the project. If she wanted to stop him she was wasting her time, but he planned to enjoy every minute they were together. For once, he had something the Conroys wanted and nothing she said or did would nudge him into changing his mind about tearing down those houses and the ghastly memories associated with them. That block along with the disgusting park bench his father called home would cease to irritate him.

But, a well thought out plan might allow him to enjoy Asa Conroy while convincing her the house had to come down. *At least I'll give it a good try.*

Chapter Two

Asa beckoned to her sister and hurried out of the auditorium. She wanted to put as much distance as possible between herself and Simeon. Standing so close to him unnerved her. His dark, piercing eyes seemed to touch her heart. The menacing demeanor from high school had vanished, replaced by a much more charismatic personality. Resisting him would take fortitude she wasn't sure she possessed.

Everyone in the room seemed to gravitate toward him, wanting his attention or simply to bask in his aura. She hadn't recognized herself as she talked with him, shifting from one foot to the next while avoiding eye contact like a nervous high school girl. The college graduate, the accomplished and composed fashion designer had disappeared.

"What's your hurry? I'm enjoying myself." Dakota rushed to keep up with Asa.

"I need some fresh air. Lots of fresh air."

"Your talk didn't go so well, huh?"

"Oh, it went just fine. We're having lunch tomorrow. Instead of barking at me the way he used to in high school, he remained very calm. I think he even stroked the palm of my hand."

"He remembers you, all right. Every time he stops in the bookstore he asks about you."

Asa stopped in mid step. "You never told me that."

Dakota hunched her shoulders. "I didn't know you

were carrying a torch for him."

"Ha. I'm not carrying a torch. That was years ago."

"The way you and Eric were always fighting, the last thing you needed to hear was some causal remark from what I thought was a high school friend. Anyway, it's good to have you home."

Dakota probably didn't mean for her comment about her marriage to jerk a knot in Asa's heart, but the result hurt just the same. Those words echoed the same sentiment expressed by her parents many times over the years. Too bad they died before seeing her make good on her talent as a designer and turning her life around.

Asa unlocked the car doors and they got inside. "I can't believe you want to stay in Mim and Pepa's house. Nobody has lived in that place for years. Are you sure everything works?"

"We'll see tonight. Thanks for having the water and electricity turned on for me. But what happened, I thought you were going to get the place cleaned?"

"Oh, yeah." Dakota snapped her seatbelt. "I forgot about that."

"Uh huh. And what about getting that ghost out of the basement too."

"Ghost?"

"Before leaving to pick you up I heard a rustling noise. I didn't try to shoo it away. You know how much I hate that basement."

"Give me a few days to clean up my place and you can

stay with me if you're afraid. We can sit up all night and catch up, like we used to do."

"Thanks, but I want to stay in the house. I need to. Why don't you spend the night with me?" Her request sounded like a plea.

"No, thanks. I've got paperwork to do tonight."

"I've been estranged from the family. Staying in the house where Mom and Dad and our grandparents lived..." She shrugged. "I'll feel closer to them. Their essence is all through that house. You understand, don't you?"

"It doesn't have to make sense to me; it only has to make sense to you. I'm just glad you're back. Remember my offer will always be open. By the time the block is leveled I'll have my spare bedroom all ready for you."

Asa gasped. "Dakota don't say that. Don't even think it. I'm going to change his mind. I have to."

Dakota shook her head. "Please don't go chasing dreams, Asa."

"I'm not. He might change his mind." Asa turned on the windshield wipers to clear the mist that had started to fall.

"Suppose he doesn't. Have you thought about that? What will you do?"

"I'm only thinking positively. There are plenty of other places he can use for his project. I only have to convince him or help find another suitable location."

Asa stopped the car in front of her sister's house and kissed her cheek. "I feel like I made a little progress tonight. I'll make a little more over lunch. So wish me luck."

"I don't know," Dakota sighed. "He's not the same man you went to school with. Simeon has a reputation for getting what he wants. He can be ruthless." Dakota said before getting out of the car.

Asa pulled away when Dakota disappeared inside the house.

He might not be the man I remembered, but I'd like to give him something he won't forget.

§ § §

Simeon sped away from the school parking lot in his Mercedes Roadster. The misting rain coated his windshield and slipped into the lowered window.

Asa Conroy had breezed back into his life just as quickly as she had disappeared. Sassy Asa still gripped his heart with a firm hold.

They were having lunch and if his luck held out, maybe more. His stomach swayed. Nothing in his life came easy, so he couldn't get excited. This wasn't just a normal date; she wanted something. If history was any predictor, whatever the Conroys wanted, they got, which meant this date could cost more than he could afford to pay.

He swung the sports car around and headed for Bristol. Facing issues head-on always worked best. The sooner he found out what Asa wanted, the sooner he could deal with the problem and move on.

Even in twilight, the same old banshees that chased him when he was too young to fight back lurked in all their familiar places. Now the housing project that he used to call home stood vacant. He smirked. In a few months, this whole neighborhood would be very different.

He drove a few more miles and turned on Excalibur Avenue. On the corner, the stately Conroy house anchored the block. He stepped out of the car and ran for the porch before adjusting his tie and squaring his shoulders. He wasn't a schoolboy anymore. Now he could talk to pretty women without getting tongue-tied.

He rang the doorbell.

Asa swung open the door. Her eyes widened. For a moment she stared without saying anything. "How did you know I was staying here?" She bent down to move a piece of luggage, from just inside the doorway. Her posture provided a clear shot of her breasts.

Simeon's back stiffened at the sight of her exposed bosom. "I took a chance."

"What about our lunch tomorrow?" she asked. Simeon swallowed the knot in his throat and averted his eyes. "We're still on for tomorrow. But I don't like surprises. You didn't stomp into my meeting tonight just to catch up with an old friend." He tried to keep his eyes on her face, but the low cut top and the tiny shorts made it difficult.

"I hear you want to tear down this grand old house." She rested her shoulder against the doorjamb. "I know it looks pretty bad right now, thanks to my well-intended sisters. But the house still has charm."

"I didn't take the personality of the house into consideration when I planned my project.

"You should have." She pushed off the doorjamb and motioned him in.

Two large pieces of luggage sat in the hall. "Are you coming or going?"

"I got into town just in time to put a stop to your plan." She sat down on the sofa and tucked her legs under her. Her shorts gave him a shot of shapely thighs and enough of her butt to make him look away.

"I doubt that." He took the chair across from her.

"Keep an open mind." She leaned forward. Her smile swept him back ten years and melted his heart.

He swallowed. "How long will you be in town?"

"I'm here to stay. I want to make this place my home."

"Isn't Bristol a little slow for you? After Atlanta, why would you want to live here again?"

"How did you know I was in Atlanta?"

"I know more about you than you can imagine." He shifted in the chair.

"Is that right? Well it seems I don't know much about you."

"In due time." He smiled. "So tell me, why did you come back?"

"This is home." She glanced around the room. "My family is here—well most of my family."

He nodded. "I was very sorry to hear about your

parents' accident. I think the whole town mourned their passing."

A pained expression crossed her face but disappeared in seconds.

He stood up. "My project is pretty well set. It's a little late to make any changes."

She unfolded her legs and stood up too. "A little late means it isn't impossible."

"I see you're still as charming as ever."

She focused on his eyes.

"I haven't even turned it on full force yet." *You don't know what you're in for.*

Chapter Three

Simeon's broad shoulders filled the entrance to the hall. A hint of stubble graced his powerful jaw. Suddenly her mind went blank. She swallowed. An unsettling flutter tickled her stomach. She trailed Simeon to the door. The hall light flickered and popped, hurling them into darkness. The only light came in from the living room.

"Sorry about that. This is the second time a light has gone out."

"Want me to change the bulb for you?" Simeon stood in the shadows, his hands deep in his pockets.

"No, I'll get it tomorrow."

"There's that sound again. That annoying rustling and scratching noise." Asa spun around. She clutched her chest and focused on the noise, but nothing could budge her to investigate the sound. The ghouls that lived in the basement could stay there forever. Even if the ghost turned out to be friendly, nothing could drag her into that black hole.

"Did you hear that?" she whispered.

"Hear what?" He stepped closer, his warm breath brushed her ear.

"I know this might sound strange, but something is living in my basement." She looked over her shoulder. "I'm not going down there."

"Are you afraid of the dark?" He placed his arm around her shoulder. Asa swayed against his solid body.

"I don't like dark, damp places. Would you mind—?"

"Not at all, show me where." He peeled off his jacket. His bulging biceps pressed against the seams of his shirt.

"It's through the kitchen." She pointed, walking behind him. The scratching noise again. It grew louder in the kitchen.

"You heard it that time, didn't you?"

"Yes, I heard something," he assured her.

Asa snatched open the pantry door expecting to find someone or something in the barren space. She found a broom, a wash pail, and a few large dust bunnies.

"You won't go in the basement, but you'll look in the pantry?" His piercing eyes challenged her.

"The basement is darker and further away from the back door."

He placed his hands on her hips. "You stand there and let me check around. Okay?" His smile softened the sharp edge in his tone. "Promise me you'll stay put."

"Okay." Asa clasped her hands and stood still. His unhurried stride slowed the anxiety crawling up her spine.

He opened the basement door, found the light switch and descended the stairs with the confidence of a knight about to slay a dragon.

Two years of celibacy had her libido in overdrive. Her skin tingled where he'd touched her hips. Wanting Simeon felt so natural. His intense gaze and that inviting smile only managed to take her back in time. A cocoon of safety enveloped her, easing the knot in her stomach. Maybe it was foolish to ask him to search the basement, but it kept him around a few more moments. Long enough to erase years of unhappiness. She rocked on her heels but stayed put.

"Do you see anything?" Asa called down the stairs.

"Not a thing. Want to come down and see for yourself?" She heard him chuckle.

"No, I'm good. I trust you." Relief blanketed her as she peered down the stairs.

Simeon emerged out of the dim lighting and climbed the steps. The set of his jaw troubled her.

"What is it?"

"Other than water in your basement, there are no bogeymen."

"Ha, ha, very funny. Is it a lot of water? Should I worry?"

"No. I can have someone come by and check it out."

"But that noise, I still hear it," Asa said. "See, there it is again. You had to hear that."

His lips curled into that crooked smile that she wanted to taste. "I hear it."

He walked to the door leading to the backyard. Her heart thumped like a conga drum.

"This used to be a safe neighborhood. What if someone's out there and charges into the room?"

"Burglars don't scratch at doors; they jimmy locks." His confidence reassured her jittery nerves.

She took a deep breath and stepped back when he

opened the door and peered into the blackness. The alley lights weren't lit and none of the neighbors bothered illuminating their back porches. A fuzzy ball charged into the kitchen and brushed her ankle.

"Ahh!" She jumped aside.

"It's okay, Asa. It's just a dog."

A scruffy puppy ran beyond her and sat near the table. The chocolate brown, long-haired dog with big, sad eyes stared back at her. Her minimal knowledge of canines told her he didn't have an AKC title, but he looked adorable.

"There's your boogeyman." Simeon knelt down to examine the animal. "He's wet from the rain, but he looks healthy."

"But what's he doing here?"

"I think you've got yourself a puppy." Simeon picked up the dog and scratched his chin. "He's cute enough. It looks like he's been abandoned. No tags or collar." He rubbed the puppy around the neck.

"Maybe he has one of those chips buried under his fur," she said.

"You can take him to the vet or SPCA to find out."

"Oh, you'll have to take him with you. You found him. My schedule is full."

"Your house, your dog." He placed the dog in her arms. "I don't do commitment. You'll make out fine. Just feed him and walk him."

"You're just going to leave me...like...this?"

"If you don't feel safe, I can stay the night." His

eyebrow shot up. "And protect you from any other four legged threats."

"No, I don't want you to leave me with this dog."

He executed a half grin and brushed his lips across her cheek. The warm touch of his luscious lips softened her resolve.

"I'll bring by a dog bone every now and then and if you ever need a sitter, I'm your man."

My man. I wish it were that easy.

§ § §

Simeon woke with a start before the alarm clock buzzed. The rhythmic tap of rain against his window was the only sound in the room. He climbed out of bed, eager to start his day. Looking forward to having lunchwith Asa.

Dreaming about her all night still had him stiff. He'd managed a few hours of sleep between the erotic dreams. He couldn't push her from his mind. The sound of her voice ran over him like warm honey. He needed his A game at lunch today unless he wanted Asa to know he still desired her. Seeing her last night only managed to stir up a yearning that had haunted him since high school. Getting entangled with Asa would bring back a lot of old memories. It would be a dumb move, he didn't do dumb anymore.

He riffled through his collection of Thomas Pink shirts and selected one with white and blue stripes to match his favorite custom-made Hugo Boss suit. He viewed his image in the dressing room mirror. After straightening his tie, he nodded approval. He wanted to impress Asa today. She needed to know Simeon Harper wasn't that poor, pathetic kid anymore. Today she'd know that the mute, adolescent idiot from school no longer existed.

She was prettier than he remembered and he remembered everything about her—those slim hips, petite waist, and large, expressive eyes. Even her dark, curly hair looked more appealing. Now she wore her beauty as if she owned it. She seemed unaware of her appeal. Her seductiveness crept under his skin. Nothing alleviated her impact.

Something always reminded him of her. A scent, a song, or even several pieces of her broken CD player that remained in a box at the back of his closet.

He drove out of the tree-lined driveway onto Route 100. Traffic grew thicker as the city drew closer. Cars crawled along Route 13 with the typical morning rush. When the light changed and he didn't make it through, he flipped to his favorite satellite jazz station. The classic sound provided a decent distraction while sitting in traffic.

§ § §

"Why the big grin? I haven't seen you this happy in the morning for months." Catherine, his assistant, sat at her desk as he rushed into his suite. She was the best administrative assistant in the firm, her organizational skills kept him sharp.

"Good morning, Catherine." He accepted a stack of documents from her. "Did you get my message about lunch?"

"Yes. Your conference room is all set up. Lunch will be delivered at noon."

"Let me know when Ms. Conroy arrives."

"The Golden Leaf contracts arrived this morning from legal. They made a few changes."

"I'll take a look at them. Also, I need you to remind me to get out of here tonight by six. If I'm in a meeting make up an excuse, but get me out."

"Not a problem." She made a note and stuck it on the corner of her desk. "Anything else?"

"Yes, make a dinner reservation for the Hotel DuPont, Green Room. Tomorrow night at seven."

She made a note on the pad. "How many?"

"Two. And I want my special corner."

In his office he opened the folder containing the Golden Leaf contract. It only took him a minute to verify that the changes he requested were included in the legal jargon. Everything was in order. His hand rested above the blank line requiring his signature. Initialing the changes altered the direction of his life. He hesitated for another moment before scribbling his initials on the contract.

The closer the project came to completion, the closer he came to fulfilling his promise to his mother. All she ever wanted was for someone to take care of the family. Her picture sat on the credenza behind his desk. Her smiling eyes settled the apprehension that prickled his spine.

He signaled for his assistant. "Catherine, please get this

paperwork to McKenna. Everything looks in order. We've worked on this for two years and it's finally coming to fruition." He exhaled with emphasis. "Tell me, where we stand with the community center contract."

Catherine accepted the folder from his outstretched hand. "Here is an extra copy for your file." She placed it on his desk. "Here is a copy of the community center project for your review. There are a few concerns with the parcel size. I know you'll be glad when they break ground on this one. It has to be your favorite project."

"This one is personal. I promised my mother I'd do something for the city. It's my gift to her."

Catherine picked up his mother's picture. "She would be very proud. If only she had lived to see it finished."

"I have to believe she's watching from that big bingo playing senior center in heaven," he joked.

His phone rang. Catherine picked it up. Her lip formed a thin line as she punched the hold button and handed the receiver to him. "It's legal. The arbitrators are here for your meeting this morning."

"Send them in." He placed the Golden Leaf contract on his desk. When the first brick of the mall was set in mortar, the hefty weight on his shoulders would lessen. The shame that visited every time he drove through his childhood neighborhood would stopping chasing him. He could drive down any street of the city and not be reminded of those difficult times. Without seeing his father draped over a park bench, too drunk to make it home, leaving his brothers and sisters to scour for food and wear hand-me-downs.

Two hours later Simeon glanced at his watch. Asa was due at his office door any minute. He stood up. "I think we're done, gentlemen. See my assistant for the documents you need. And let's touch base in a few weeks."

He opened the door and spotted Asa sauntering down the hall. Her unbelievable beauty sent heat rolling across his flesh. The miniskirt hugging her slim hips revealed the sexiest pair of legs in the state. His body jerked to life.

He shook hands with the departing entourage and rushed to greet her.

"I take it you slept well since I extricated your ghost." He kissed her hand. "And you're right on time."

"Let me tell you how hard it was with that dog. I called every animal shelter in Bristol to see if anyone was looking for the little critter. I even knocked on a few of my neighbors' doors to see if they could identify him."

"Any luck?"

"Well the kid down the block offered to help me. We took a picture with my cell phone and he promised to put some flyers around the neighborhood. I should have brought the puppy along today so he could entertain you."

"I can tell you love him already. It's a perfect match." He led her into the conference room. Their lunch graced the table's elegant setting. Catherine never disappointed.

Asa's crisp cologne tickled his nose as he held the chair for her. "You smell as good as you look."

"Are you just saying that so that I don't deposit that adorable puppy on your doorstep?"

"Not at all. He's my excuse to pop over for a visit."

"You don't need an excuse." She placed her chin in her palm and leaned closer. "I just hope there's a place for you to pop into. There's an evil villain threatening to blow my house down."

"Ah, and now the reason for our meeting. But even bad guys have a few good qualities." He removed the lids from the platters.

"Is that right? Like what?"

"Let's eat first then I'll listen to everything you want to say."

Her eyes lit up, sparkling like diamonds. "I need you to do more than listen."

"And what do I get out of this deal?" He stared into her eyes, willing her to break the chains keeping them apart.

"Well, what do you want?"

You.

Chapter Four

Asa closed her eyes and rubbed her temples. Mim always said be careful what you pray for, cause you just might get it. Maybe allowing Simeon to tear down the house had an upside. She took a deep calming breath before opening her eyes again. The jagged hole in the ceiling remained as did the plaster on the floor.

Her phone chimed from her nightstand. She leaned the mop against the wall, grabbed the phone and scanned the screen. Simeon's named flashed in capital letters.

"Simeon, how are you?" she cooed into the phone, happy to be relieved of clean-up duty even for just a moment.

"I enjoyed our lunch yesterday." His sexy baritone vibrated in her ear.

Yesterday they had talked about everything but the house over lunch. After filling her in on all their classmates, he talked about his projects. His eyes sparkled with excitement, as he described each one.

"I did too. It was fun. Your stories had me cracking up. I had no idea our senior class president wanted to open up a brothel in Bristol, of all places."

"Oh, I've got a lot more stories. I'll share them over dinner, tonight?"

"I'm looking forward to it. But I want you to know, I'm onto your plan."

"My plan?"

"Aren't you trying to distract me so I won't pressure

you about the house? You know with all the wining and dining stuff?"

His deep laughter resounded through the phone, making her smile. "Umm, I hadn't thought about it, but that sound like a good plan." He paused for a moment. She could hear him breathing. "I've got a late meeting, so I hope you don't mind meeting me there."

"It's not a problem. I've got some stuff to take care of this morning." She eyeballed the pile of wet plaster in the middle of the hall. "See you there at seven." Asa disconnected the call.

Heat raced through her veins like an out of control fire. Simeon's infectious charm ignited the dry tinder buried in her heart. The spark had already begun to mushroom.

"Hey, where are you?" Dakota called from downstairs. The dog released a loud yap as he charged out of the room. His barking grew fiercer as he neared the stairs.

"Up here, come on up." Asa responded before reaching for the mop.

She watched Dakota's lip curl in dissatisfaction. Scruffy's barking only added to the chaos.

"When did you get a dog?" Dakota stood in the upstairs hallway with her hands on her hips.

"This is my ghost. I adopted him a few nights ago."

"Can't you shut him up?"

"He doesn't like strangers." Asa made a wide swipe with the mop.

"You were a stranger to him until a few nights ago.

Give me a break."

"I'm kinda getting used to having him around. It's a good thing, too because the animal shelter says he doesn't have a chip and no one has any idea where he came from."

"I saw the flyers pinned to the trees as I drove up the block. Maybe you'll get a response." Dakota pointed to the water and plaster on the floor. "Now, what happened here?"

"I wish you called me before you dropped by." Asa continued to mop up the water. "I would have asked you to buy trash bags to put this stuff in."

"Are you going to tell me what's going on here?" Scruffy gave Dakota another growl before running into the bedroom.

"The roof leaks. The ceiling fell in from the weight of the water. What in the world am I getting into here? The house is a wreck."

"Umm hm, I told you this wasn't a good idea. How are you going to stay here? Are you crazy?"

Asa swallowed her sharp retort. Instead she said, "Are you going to help me clean up this mess or are you going to stand there and watch me? I have an appointment downtown with a realtor."

Dakota snatched the broom leaning against the wall. "I'm going to try to talk some sense into your head." She pushed the soaking wet plaster into a pile. "You go from one harebrained scheme to the next. Why don't you just come and stay with me?"

Asa chuckled. Dakota was always the messy one. "It's

just a little rain, Dakota."

"Today it's rain, tomorrow the walls might cave in, or the floor might buckle. Honey, maybe this house can't be saved. Have you thought about that?"

"Nope, not once."

"What about Simeon? Has he said anything positive?"

"Nope, not once," she repeated. Asa stopped mopping. With one hand she swept her hair away from her face. "Let's see... where do I start. I've seen him twice, we're having dinner tonight at the most expensive restaurant in the city and he still hasn't shown his hand. The house is still on the chopping block."

"He invited you to dinner tonight. That sounds pretty serious to me." Dakota made a large swipe with the broom.

"If he's serious, he has a funny way of showing it. So far he's given me a brotherly hug or a simple kiss on the cheek. I think all this attention has more to do with letting me know he doesn't intend to change his plans."

"Don't be silly. He could have said that on a phone call, he's got something on his mind. You." She lifted a brow.

Asa shook her head. "Don't give me that look. I know what I'm talking about."

Dakota leaned the broom against the wall. "Besides this manual labor, what can I help with?"

"I might need help finding the best location for my studio. The realtor has several properties for me to look at this afternoon." She glanced at her watch. "If I don't take my shower and get out of here I'm going to be late. Don't you want to take Scruffy for a little walk so he can handle his business?"

"Not on your life. I don't do dogs." Dakota scurried down the stairs. "Good luck with Simeon tonight."

Asa laughed hearing the door close.

§ § §

Asa drummed her fingers on the plush linen tablecloth. Her first dinner in the Hotel DuPont Green Room and she couldn't take her eyes off the gold gilded ceiling or the elegant decor. A woman played a harp on the small balcony overlooking the dining room. The heavy brocade drapes over the large domed windows blended well with the room décor.

Simeon was late.

Why would he pick one of the most expensive restaurants in Wilmington for dinner? She fumbled with the place setting before running her hands along her black crepe peplum dress.

The blaring alarms from passing fire engines barely penetrated the serene surroundings of the dining room. Everyone continued to eat and drink, ignoring the emergency vehicles outside.

She glanced at the list of exquisite entrees trying to choose one before Simeon arrived. This way he wouldn't have to witness her indecisiveness.

"Ma'am, would you like to order a drink while you're waiting?"

"Mmm, yes, I guess so." Around the restaurant, tables were filling up. The noise level increased two octaves. Why would Simeon keep her waiting so long? "I'll have a sour apple martini." Before he could walk away, she raised her hand. "No, no make that a desert pear martini."

The server nodded and hurried away. The host escorted a middle-aged couple across the dining room. Their arms were linked at the elbow. They reminded Asa of her parents and the love they shared.

The phone in her purse vibrated. After fishing around, she pulled it out and noticed Eric's number illuminating the screen. Instead of taking the call she silenced the ringer and slipped the phone back in her purse. The love she'd thought she and Eric had shared faded before their first year was through. He'd get the message soon enough.

She craned her neck looking for the server with the martini. He was just arriving. She accepted the delicate stemmed glass from the server and took a long swallow before setting it on the table. Asa squeezed her eyes shut for fortification as the vodka slid down her throat.

From this side of the dining room, she couldn't track the activity at the entrance. Each time the host escorted someone to their seat Asa glanced up to see if Simeon had arrived. He was twenty minutes late. If this meeting wasn't so important she would drop some money on the table and walk out. Ten more minutes. She would give him ten more minutes to show up.

She suppressed a smile, if sitting a few more moments

guaranteed her some time with Simeon then she was content to wait. She swung her foot to the slow melody of the harp and took another sip of her drink. The next gulp of her martini didn't require a squint.

She finished the rest of the drink then pulled her pocketbook off the back of the chair. She extracted twenty dollars from her wallet, placed it on the table and raced toward the exit. If Simeon thought she would give up this easy, she had a surprise for him.

Two could play this game.

Chapter Five

Her Mercedes rattled and lurched as she pulled onto 10th Street. Maybe the car needed a tune up. After the long drive from Atlanta, the eight year old vehicle deserved a rest.

"Hold on until after the studio is opened, then it will be your turn." She patted the dashboard.

The sun faded from the sky as she turned onto the old family block. The full oak trees made a canopy across the street. It felt like driving under a leaf-covered arch. There was something magical about this street, about this house. Her grandparents' house stood in marked contrast to the beauty of the trees on the block. Tomorrow she vowed to get the yard cleaned up. To bring the house back to some resemblance of its glory.

Once inside the house, she turned on all of the lights. Scruffy ran out of the kitchen, his tail wagging so violently his whole backside shook. She scratched under his chin. "God, it feels good to have someone happy to see me." She picked up the puppy, rubbed his nose against hers then sat him on the floor.

"This house needs a little tender loving care. Just like me," she said to Scruffy as he licked his paw.

She stifled a yawn while the dog gobbled up his kibble. Her phone vibrated again, startling her. It was Eric again. Twice in one night. He hadn't showed that much interest when they were married, so what made her the center of attention now? She pushed the phone back in her pocket and headed upstairs with the dog in her arms.

The cold brass doorknob of her grandparents' bedroom filled her trembling hand. She squared her shoulders before pushing the door open. After two nights, she needed to peek into the room to see the big bed where her grandparents let her sleep after a bad dream.

Asa gripped the doorjamb, her feet refused to move forward. With Scruffy squeezed against her chest her eyes darted around the room. It looked exactly the way she remembered. Her grandmother's comb still sat on the dresser. The large four-poster bed faced the door. The patchwork quilt that she and her sisters used to build their playhouse was still draped across the corner of the bed. The room looked as if Mim had made the bed only that morning.

She inched forward and took a deep breath hoping to smell the inexpensive perfume her grandmother wore, or the tobacco from her Grandfather's pipe. But the musty smell that permeated the rest of the house laid claim to this room as well.

§ § §

Three hours. Three excruciating hours, his millwright would be fine but a fractured arm should not take three hours to set. Simeon pulled his car out of the hospital parking lot and headed toward Interstate 95 South.

His presence had helped diffuse the uneasiness of the crew. They needed to know how much he cared about them and their families.

Building Harper Enterprise took several years and even

more years of sacrifice. Giving up his time or changing his schedule all came along as part of the package. His father never understood anything about sacrifice, which reflected in the lifestyle he chose for his family. Give him a bottle of cheap wine and Nolan Harper was as content as a dog getting his belly scratched.

But this wasn't the day he wanted to sacrifice his personal life for his business. He shifted in the car seat. Before today, nothing came before Harper Enterprise and certainly not a woman. He smirked, if anyone could make him push business aside, Asa would be the one.

"Call Catherine," he spoke into the car's voice command and waited for Catherine to pick up.

"Simeon, I got to the Green Room as quickly as I could. An accident or a fire or something had traffic tied up for blocks. By the time I got there, Ms. Conroy was gone."

"Did you call the restaurant? Does she know something came up?"

"I'm sorry Simeon. I didn't get a message to her. I didn't think...I...I'm sorry."

"Don't worry about it, Catherine. I'll handle it." He disconnected the call.

Traffic through Chester, Pennsylvania along I-95 slowed. He inched along, strumming the steering wheel to channel his anxiety. Something always happened to keep him away from Asa.

Even now, success didn't seem to be enough to bring him closer to her. The money, the large house, his own business and he still wasn't any closer to Asa than when they were in high school. Somehow she remained beyond his grasp.

He swung around a slow moving car and accelerated. The dashboard clock read ten. He seldom paid house calls this late, but he needed to see Asa tonight. Sleeping would be impossible until he made certain she understood what kept him from dinner.

Finding his way to the house on Excalibur Avenue didn't pose a challenge. He could find it in the dark, with a blindfold covering his eyes. Even the condition of the house wasn't surprising. Before planning the Golden Leaf project he had ridden down this street every day. Since no one lived in her house or took care of the repairs, his decision was easier. Her house, her neighborhood reminded him of everything painful in his childhood. It was the constant reminder that his father loved the bottle more than he loved his family.

Now Asa wanted to *talk* about his project. As much as he adored her and wanted her, she wouldn't change his plans. He'd made too many promises

Promises I plan to keep.

Chapter Six

The doorbell jarred Asa awake. She bolted upright in the bed. The dog barked. His body rigid at the foot of the bed. He sounded like a ferocious pit bull instead of a small mutt. She checked the time on her cell phone. Eleven o'clock. It felt later. Only a handful of people knew she'd moved into the house, but none of them would visit at this hour.

Asa burrowed under the blanket. If she stayed upstairs, maybe whoever was at the door would go away. The doorbell rang again. This time Scruffy hopped off the bed and bolted down the stairs.

"Scruffy, come back here." Asa ran after the puppy, turning on the hall light as she made her way down the steps. She scooped the puppy into her arms just as the bell chimed again.

"Well, I guess we can't hide now, can we? The jig is up, thanks to you," she admonished the puppy.

Through the door side panels, she saw Simeon, dressed in a suit, looking as fresh as a brand new day.

"Oh, shit," Asa whispered as she dropped the curtain covering the panel. She put the dog on the floor. Her hair must looked like she stuck her finger in an electrical socket and her gown almost exposed her butt. She threw up her hand. Why do I care what Simeon thinks? That freak stood me up tonight and now he has the nerve to show up here.

She snatched the door open. "I've invited you to this house a dozen times and the only time you show up is when I don't invite you. Are you serious?" she lashed out at him. Scruffy continued to bark but now he stood behind her. Some guard dog. Simeon's wide stance bordered on menacing. His hands were shoved in his pockets. From the porch's dim light, she couldn't easily make out the expression on his face. He almost looked like a detective that had come to arrest her for having too much mouth. She gave him a moment to reply. When he didn't, she continued. "You have some nerve. Do you have any idea what time it is?"

"I felt like I owed you an apology. I'm sorry about tonight, there was an accident at one of the job sites and I had to go to the hospital. I tried to call your cell, it went directly to voicemail." His eyes traveled the length of her body and stopped at the end of her gown.

Calm down. He's only looking, the same way any hot blooded man would.

"You don't look hurt to me." She eyed him.

"Do you always have such a quick wit?"

"Only after ten o'clock. It's my Cinderella thing."

"I thought Cinderella's bewitching hour was midnight." His lip curled into a seductive smile that made

Asa forget her anger for a moment. "Yeah, well, I need my sleep."

"I'll make a note of that."

"Does that mean you'll keep coming back after my lights are out?"

"Again, I'm sorry." He explained the accident to her.

"Can I come in for a moment?" He removed his hands from his pockets.

Asa stepped aside allowing him in the hall where the light to shine on his face. She looked into his eyes, the black flecks danced against the hazy hall light. "I was sleeping..."

"I'll only be a few minutes." His deep voice went right to her heart, making it beat faster. He brushed against her as he stepped into the hall. His touch sent a current through her along with the realization that she was nearly naked, her nipples hardening against the thin fabric. She tugged on the gown.

Without moving he glanced into the living room. He seemed to fill the space, reminding her of her father and grandfather and their bigger than life presences. Before he uttered another word, she forgave him for standing her up.

"I'm listening." She tried to sound indifferent. Scruffy stopped barking and wandered closer to Simeon. After sniffing his pants, he sat on the worn carpet.

"It's not often that I allow work to interfere with my private life. I hope you can forgive me. We're facing some tough challenges right now and I need to make sure my crews feel my support."

"You didn't need to come here tonight. You could have called me in the morning. I look a mess." She pulled her hair up to fashion a ponytail.

"You've never looked a mess." He cleared this throat and dropped his gaze. "I sent my assistant to the restaurant to take care of your dinner and let you know I wasn't going to make it, but you had already left."

Asa clutched her gown closer to her chest. "Oh, so you do know how to be nice. That makes twice."

"You keep count?"

"It's pretty easy with you. You're up to two. You chased the ghost out of the basement and treated me to a nice lunch." She held up two fingers. "This Simeon is much better than the one I went to school with."

He arched a brow. "I...hope so. Hey wait a minute. I invited you to dinner tonight." His electric smile sent a shiver across her skin.

"You invited me to dinner, and then you blew me off. I wouldn't brag about that if I were you."

Instead of commenting, he stared. A tingle traveled down her spine, enveloping her. She wanted to touch him, feel the warmth of his skin along his jaw. A static charge surrounded them. The blood rushing through her veins threatened to spring a leak and leave her useless in the middle of the hall.

She needed to deflect his penetrating gaze. "The way I figure it, you owe me a dinner and a CD player."

"A CD Player?"

"You broke the one my father gave me for my birthday."

"Are you sure it was me? When did I break your CD player?"

"The last week of school in our senior year, you smacked it out of my hand. And yes, I'm sure it was you."

She could still feel the sting of that moment.

He changed his stance. "That sounds pretty awful."

"You were pretty awful back then. At least you were awful to me. And I've been home a little over forty-eight hours and you're still batting a thousand."

"I guess I owe you two apologies then." His mouth curled into a charming smile. "And I'd like to start by taking you out to dinner. One that I won't miss. Tomorrow night. Can I pick you up at six?"

"Do you really intend on picking me up or is this just another one of your tactics to wear me down and have me go away?"

"You don't seem like the kind of woman that wears down easily."

She licked her lips and smiled. "You're so different...from high school."

He smiled. "Different how?"

Her heart leaped in her chest while her brain tried to articulate a response. "Back then you only grunted, you never said a civil word to me. And I didn't think your face knew how to smile."

"So, it's a good change?" Simeon looked down at her, his lips were only inches away from her face. Calm down Asa. Back away from his lips.

She dropped her head. "I'm withholding judgment until I get more data."

"Fair enough. Then what about dinner?" he asked again.

"This is the first time you've asked me out."

"I asked you out tonight."

"It doesn't count since you blew me off."

"Okay. So you can't turn me down now that I'm trying to make it up to you."

She searched his face without answering for a long moment. Was he the enemy or a friend? He wanted to destroy the house. "I guess so. And are you admitting that you were awful to me in high school?"

"I'm smart enough to plead the fifth on that." His eyes traveled up her legs. "But, I'm not leaving here tonight unless you promise to give me another chance."

She crossed her legs, pinning them together so tightly she almost lost her balance. "Okay, let's give it one more try." She smiled.

He held her hand. "I'm really sorry about tonight. And I promise to pick you up promptly for our next date." He looked into her eyes.

Date? When had they started dating? Her plan to seduce him was going woefully awry. Scruffy ran up to her and yelped.

"I think someone wants your attention." Simeon nodded at the dog.

"It figures. He probably thinks it's morning and time to go for a walk."

Simeon turned and glanced out the window. "In this neighborhood you need to be careful walking this late at night."

"Are you kidding me? This neighborhood is fantastic. It's safe. Anyway, I usually just open the back door and let him scoot outside."

"You haven't been here in a few years. The area isn't like you remember. I'll walk with you and—"

"Scruffy. I named him Scruffy. And why would you want to walk with us? Don't you have some important thing to run off to?"

"Let's just say I owe you. Besides, I'm still pretty tense about the site accident. Walking will help me de-stress."

"I need to dress first." She hesitated, thinking he would change his mind and go home.

"I'll wait."

§ § §

He enjoyed the glimpse of her butt as she charged up the stairs. His penis stiffened as blood rushed through his loins. "Shit," he uttered as he adjusted his stance.

He paced the small entranceway to manage his erection. She looked fantastic; her raw beauty made his pulse race. He wanted to scoop her up in his arms, kiss her soft lips, and run his tongue over her nipples that peeked through the nightgown, making it hard for him to raise his eyes above her chest. Instead of just dreaming of Asa, she had stood within inches of him, with only a flimsy scrap of fabric between him and her bare skin. He wanted her more than any woman he had ever met.

In the living room the frayed furniture, thin rug, and old

fixtures showed their age. The walls needed a good coat of paint, but he could easily see the majesty the house had once possessed. As a boy, the house seemed huge, now it didn't appear nearly as large or as stately.

He poked his head into the dining room and glanced in the kitchen. The light in the hall flickered, pitching him into darkness for a moment before coming back on.

Compared to the shack he grew up in, this place still resembled Buckingham Palace but it was far less threatening now.

Upstairs the hardwood floors creaked under her weight. The vision of her curvy body and cascading curls as she disappeared up the stairs flashed in his mind. He devoured every detail, dissecting her like a laboratory animal. To ease his erection, he switched his thoughts to the dog sitting at the base of the stairs. The dog whined for Asa. Simeon picked him up and rubbed his head. "Yeah, buddy, she has that effect on men."

Asa bounded down the stairs wearing tight fitting yoga pants and a tank top without a bra. Her breasts still taunting him. Her ponytail looked a little more managed but several tendrils still hung loose. "I'm ready."

"Aren't you going to wear shoes?"

"No, I'm just going a few blocks. Besides it's warm outside. I never wear shoes in the summer."

"I think you'll need them tonight. It's dark and there may be glass. I don't want to make another trip to the hospital today."

"Simeon," she said his name like no one else. It

sounded like a song the way she pronounced it. Her mischievous smile was hard to resist. Everything about her only heightened his senses and stirred up emotions he thought were buried years ago. He wanted to be angry with her and her family, but he couldn't hold to it when she smiled or said his name.

He chuckled at the pout she gave him before running upstairs.

She returned a moment later wearing a pair of flip-flops.

"You call those shoes?"

"It's the best you're going to get tonight. Let's go."

Simeon turned away and suppressed a groan when she bent over to leash the dog, exposing part of her thong and the small of her back. The tight pants did little to conceal her butt. "Let me leave my jacket here." He removed his jacket and placed it on the banister before following her out the door.

She determined the direction of their stroll. He rolled up his sleeves as they meandered from one block to the next without talking.

"I think you better have the electricity checked. Do you know your lights flicker?"

"As soon as I can convince you to leave my house alone, I'll get a contractor in."

"I see you've placed flyers all over the place," he pointed to the bright sheet tacked to a tree.

"I guess I'm now the proud owner of this mutt. The

shelter said dog owners that are looking for their pets usually show up pretty quickly. I'll give it another week, then I'll take the notices down."

Simeon nodded. After a few moments he asked. "So, tell me about your husband, where is he?"

"Ex-husband, and he's still in Atlanta. We're divorced, two years now." She hunched her shoulders. "My marriage didn't work out so I decided to move back here, to be with my family, where my roots are."

"I see." Simeon shoved his hands in his pockets. Now he understood why she wanted to meet with him. He decided to put his question out there. "So about the house. What did you want to say?"

"If we talk now, does that mean you're off the hook for dinner tomorrow?"

"No, not at all," he smirked. "I didn't want you to have to wait until tomorrow."

Asa stopped while Scruffy smelled a tree box. "I wanted to talk to you about your project. I hope there is an alternative. A way to save the block." She pulled on the leash.

A car engine came to life down the street. A quick flash from the high beams blinded him for a moment. Simeon waited until the driver pulled away to respond. "I see."

"That house...that house has so many memories for me and my whole family. My sisters and I grew up there. My parents were married in the living room and after they were killed my grandparents planted a tree in the backyard in honor of them. That tree is still there and it's, it's..." She paused. "The block parties...remember the yearly summer block parties? The whole neighborhood came."

"Not the whole neighborhood," Simeon grunted. The Harper family never attended one of those parties.

She studied his face for a moment. "You could have, but you were always so…so..."

"So what?"

"You were always so serious. You didn't have time for fun."

"Is that what you think?"

She tugged on the dog's leash. "You never led me to think anything else."

Neither of them spoke for several seconds.

"Nearly everyone came to those parties. They lasted well into the night. I remember all the food, everyone laughing and having a good time," Asa's voice sounded cheerful. "That's why I needed to come back here after the divorce. This is home, it always has been. The house is great and there is no way anyone can live in that house and not be happy."

Simeon gnashed his teeth. Hearing her cheery chatter about the fabulous summer block parties and the grand old house made him tense. The house he grew up in was the exact opposite. Bickering and fighting for food with his siblings were the highlighted activities. Being excluded from the one thing that the whole town talked about all summer only reinforced his alienation. As soon as that block came down, so would his awful memories.

"You are a persistent little cuss. Like that dog with his bone. No matter how many times I say no, you keep coming back, don't you."

Asa stopped walking. "It's my plan to wear you down. I can be pretty persuasive."

"I'll say. And I keep trying to ply you with food to get you thinking about something else. I can come up with so many other things for us to do."

"I thought you just enjoyed my company." She smiled.

"That too. I definitely enjoy spending time with you." If he squelched her idea right now, there wouldn't be any excuse to spend time with her. The houses on that block were coming down and the sooner he did it the better. He cleared this throat. "But, I'm not promising anything with the house."

"I just want you to think about it." Her smile made him feel better, but not good enough to change his plans.

"Good boy, Scruffy," she said to the dog as he relieved himself against a tree. "I think we can head back now."

She pivoted on her heel and turned back toward her house. Simeon didn't want the walk to end. After hours spent on the hard chairs in the waiting room and the grueling traffic back to Bristol, this time with her salvaged his day. He wanted a little more, but Scruffy pulled her down the block. Simeon stepped up beside her.

"That was a short walk."

"He's pretty easy to please, a little food, a short walk, and a rub on the belly makes him happy. Too bad everyone isn't that easy to please."

"Maybe they are. You just have to get the right combination."

"Sometimes there is no right combination. I should know. That's why I'm divorced and if I ever marry again it's going to be perfect. My sisters are waiting for me to fall on my face. They think investing money in the house is a colossal mistake. I don't think they even support the idea of me opening a studio here." She stopped in front of the stairs.

Simeon placed his foot on the first step and watched Asa and Scruffy walk up the stairs to the door. Her sanctuary, his nightmare.

"I hope you think about what I've said."

He barely heard her comment. Her ponytail had come loose and curls fell to her shoulders. Tonight was the most they'd ever talked. The unexpected intimacy made it hard for him to say goodnight. His senses were in overdrive. He watched her lips move and wanted to taste her. Every muscle in his body ached to hold her, touch her.

He climbed the stairs. "I see you still have the same tenacity you possessed in high school."

She looked up at him. Her eyes were as bright as the stars. She mumbled something but the words floated away in the night air.

"I guess I better get inside." She didn't move.

He continued to hold her gaze. "Asa—" the porch light popped, leaving them in the shadows. The spell was broken. Simeon quashed the sigh that rose in his throat. He'd get another chance. "I think you might have to replace several light bulbs."

"It's on my list of things to do." She unlocked the door and pushed it open. She flipped the hall switch and nothing happening. "I'm going to need a dozen bulbs."

Simeon placed his hand on her back and followed her into the house. Her warmth heightened his desire. Pushing his tongue in her mouth seemed a fitting place to start. She walked into the living room and stumbled over the coffee table before finding the lamp switch. It clicked but the light did not come on.

He glanced out the window. "I think it's just your house, all of your neighbors seem to have electricity."

Asa plopped down on the stairs. The dull haze from the streetlight outside provided only a band of light. She looked so tiny sitting in the darkness. Her dog looked up at her, then sat at her feet.

"I don't know if I have no electricity because Dakota failed to pay the bill, or if I've got a much larger issue." Asa released the leash and dropped her hand.

"Well you can't stay here tonight."

"I better starting looking for a hotel that takes dogs, because going to Dakota's is out of the question."

"Stay with me. You can stay with me." The words slipped out so easily, they surprised him. Overnight guests were a rarity. Women only stayed long enough to share a night of pleasure. But this invitation offered no such benefit. Having Asa under his roof sure seemed like a benefit, but the ramifications could be colossal. Nothing about her said one night stand. Asa was the girl you married and forged a life with. Maybe she should stay in one of his other properties, not under his roof. He adjusted his stance. Asa stared at him, her sexy mouth slightly parted.

Before she could reject his offer, he moved closer. "I have plenty of room. And you and your dog...Scruffy can stay as long as you want."

"Why? Why would you make such an offer? We haven't spoken since high school."

"To hear you tell it, as mean as I was to you in high school, I owe you."

Her lip trembled. She wiped her tear before it ran down her cheek. "Suppose I take you up on your offer?"

"I hope you do. You can't stay here in the dark." He watched while she contemplated his offer. His heart pushed against his chest like a horse at the starting gates.

She searched his face before running up the stairs. "Okay, I'm coming."

God, I hope so.

Chapter Seven

Asa slid behind the driver's seat of her car. Deciding to drive to his house made her feel just a bit better about accepting the offer. The drive to Simeon's house blurred into a flash of passing scenery. Asa's thoughts raced through the conversation leading up to his invitation. The vision of Simeon standing in her front hall wouldn't leave her brain. All the promises to remain focus, to stay away from men until after the shop opened, evaporated when his touch singed her flesh.

"Okay, Scruffy, you haven't known me long but believe me, this is one of the dumbest things I've ever done. It's right up there with marrying Eric. My whole plan to seduce him could backfire in my face." Asa nibbled her bottom lip.

She pulled into the driveway behind Simeon.

His brick mansion secured a hill overlooking the Delaware Valley. Rose bushes cozied up to the house along both sides of the front door. His plush hillside acreage welcomed her. Staying in Simeon's house seemed like a good idea on the way across town, but as he motioned her into the garage, she wasn't so sure. Her stomach tightened into a hard knot. Was this visit only because she had no electricity? Or was this another opportunity to spend time with him?

Two years of celibacy and his touch had her libido in overdrive. Wanting Simeon was so natural. His intense gaze and those piercing eyes took her back in time validating her high school instincts. Everything about him exuded sex, charm, and irresistibility made her want to jump his bones. Maybe during the night she could feign sleepwalking and end up in his bedroom.

She grabbed Scruffy's leash and stepped out of the car. "Wow, Simeon, this is a nice place, it's huge." She looked around. "You're sure my dog and I aren't imposing?"

"Come on in, Asa. There's plenty of room."

He ran his hand across the small of her back. This time the warmth of his touch radiated along her spine and settled in her core. Staying in his house was going to be as challenging as trying to save hers.

Asa kissed his cheek. "Thank you."

Before she could pull away, he drew her closer, pressing her body against his steel chest. He captured her mouth and teased her tongue for a moment before beginning a full on assault. Forgetting the house, her shop, and the fashion show, she surrendered to the liquefied heat surging through her veins. His hand entangled in her hair, drawing her closer. Then he released her before she was sated.

"Let's get inside." His voice sounded thick with lust. He removed her bag from the trunk.

She suppressed a moan and followed him from the garage into the mud room. I just kissed Simeon and he kissed me back. He kissed me. Her brain moved at warp speed. This should not have happened. She fumbled with the leash, nearly tripping over the dog. His taste lingered in her mouth. She rolled her tongue along her lips, still feeling the pressure from his touch.

A dim light illuminated the enormous kitchen.

Without turning on more lights Simeon set her bag down and walked to the refrigerator.

"My housekeeper is a very good cook, I'm sure there are some leftovers in the fridge. Care to join me." He sat several casserole dishes on the counter and removed the lids.

"After being stood up, I went home and ate a pint of ice cream. Chocolate."

"That hardly sounds nutritional."

Simeon pulled two plates from the cabinet. After loading lamb chops, garlic mashed potatoes and broccoli au gratin on two separate plates he took turns heating them in the microwave.

"I wasn't looking for healthy, I wanted yummy. This smells good though and you do owe me dinner." Asa pulled her stool closer to the counter.

The heavy clang of cutlery as he placed it on the granite started her stomach juice churning. He slid wineglasses from the overhead grid in the butler's pantry and with three swift moves popped the cork on a bottle of Merlot.

"You know your way around the kitchen, don't you?" She asked.

"I had to learn at an early age. Being slow when it was time to eat could mean no dinner." He handed her a glass of wine. "How about you, can you cook?"

"I do all right. But ask me to bake something special and I'm all over it."

"It's late tonight, so I won't challenge you." He bent his tall frame down and met her at eye level. His lips were inches from her mouth. By leaning forward she could lock lips with him, instead she grounded her hips to the stool.

"So you do the sweet thing, huh. Pies, cakes, cookies?"

"Oh, I do way more than that. I'll have to prepare one of my specialties for you."

Asa scooted forward, without diverting her eyes away from his mouth. One more taste of his succulent lips and the day would go down in her journal as perfect. Her lips were still warm from his earlier kiss. She couldn't tear her eyes away his touch had fueled a desire in her that needed release.

The microwave sounded and he broke eye contact. Asa pulled in a deep breath before taking a big swallow from her glass.

He removed the plates from the microwave and sat next to her at the counter. "Dig in," he said as he sliced the meat.

The hearty plate in front of her smelled delicious. She tasted a forkful of mashed potatoes. The pungent taste of garlic filled her mouth. "These potatoes are divine."

"Ruthy is a good cook." He poured more wine in her glass, tapped his glass to hers and sipped his wine. "Are you worried about your house?"

"Since I got home, the house has had one problem after the next. Nothing will surprise me now. I'll make some calls in the morning."

"No need. I called one of my guys to check it out in the

morning."

"You have guys? And when did you have time to make these arrangements."

"I own a company and I made a call on the drive here. Try not to worry. If it's something that can be fixed then he'll make the repair."

"But how will he get in the house?" Asa ate another forkful of potatoes.

"He's going to stop by here on his way to your house tomorrow."

"You got it all planned. I should thank you," she hesitated. "Thank you."

He nodded.

Having someone looking out for her is all she ever wanted. Most times it seemed too much to ask or to expect. Simeon's easy-going magnetism was hypnotic. Eating dinner next to him, the causal flow of conversation, seemed about as perfect as the sun rising in the east.

After several moments of silence Asa asked, "So why does a single man need such a big house? Are there any little Simeons running around that you haven't told me about?"

His playful smile brightened his eyes. He put his fork down turned to face her. "There are no little Simeons. Yet. Are you applying for the job?"

She ignored the tingle between her legs. Hell, yeah! "I don't know. Does it pay well?" She teased.

"Very well."

She tried to swallow, but her tongue wouldn't move. "Are you trying to seduce me, Simeon?" She picked up her glass and sipped the wine.

"Only if it's working."

"Let's see, good food, good wine, beautiful surrounding, one gorgeous man. I'd say that's a recipe for the ultimate seduction."

"I hope you find my charm as captivating as I find you." His eyes darkened, lust sparkled in the depth of his pupils.

"Very." She had to push words out. Warning signs buzzed in her head. She squelched her enthusiasm. *Finish what you've started this time. The studio, the show, the house. Show your family you're not a screw-up.*

She pushed away from the counter and stood up. "I'm full. I better take the dog out and get ready for bed."

§ § §

Simeon released a long breath and watched her disappear into the darkness with her dog close behind. Denying any attraction to her made about as much sense as denying his arousal from the moment he stepped into her house.

He placed the dishes in the dishwasher. His luck had turned. Even his skilled hand couldn't have manipulated this situation any better. Her lights going out played right into his hands. Now all he had to do was coax her into his bed.

All those years thinking about her and not being able to tell her how he felt. He shook his head, so much wasted time. He wiped his brow and reached for his glass of wine. She looked flushed as she allowed the dog to enter the kitchen ahead of her.

"Are you okay?" Simeon crossed the room.

"Yes. But do you know you have deer in your yard? That thing scared the bejesus out of me!"

He gave her a playful hug. "Next time, I'll go with you and Scruffy to keep you safe. It seems my new task is protecting you."

She didn't pull away, so he allowed his hand to roll across her shoulder and down her arm. Her skin was baby soft. He dropped his hand, returned to the table and emptied his glass of wine with one long swallow.

"Let me show you where you're sleeping tonight," he said after picking up her bags. He led the way upstairs and dropped her bags in the bedroom at the top of the stairs.

"Maybe it's a good thing I hadn't unpacked. Mim used to say every cloud has a silver lining."

"I guess so." He glanced over his shoulder. "I want you to feel comfortable so you can stay at one end of the hall. The master suite is on the other side of the house."

"Is that for my benefit or yours?"

"It's for your benefit." He smiled and walked out. *Trust me.*

Chapter Eight

The morning sun filtered through the thin gauze curtains. Asa stretched her legs under the soft cotton sheets and rubbed her eyes.

"Scruffy, I'm sleeping with the enemy. Or in his house at least."

During the night, sleep had come in between fits of passion. Every few minutes an erotic scene of Simeon and all the lusty things she wanted them to do. The penetrating warmth of his hand lingered on her flesh. She woke up more exhausted than when she went to bed.

Asa flipped on her side, the comfort of the king sized mattress was hard to resist. The dog jumped to attention at the foot of the bed and stared at the door. He started to bark so Asa sat up, resting on her elbows. She heard footsteps in the hall.

Simeon knocked on the door. "Asa, are you awake? Can I come in?"

She tightened the sheet over her breasts. Before responding she ran her fingers through her hair, fluffing the curls. "Yes, come in."

He opened the door and strode across the room carrying a tray of orange juice and croissants. His unbuttoned shirt exposed his rippled chest. Asa refrained from the urge to lick her lips. She focused her attention on his taut bronze stomach.

"You're still in bed, didn't you sleep well?"

"I slept like a baby." She looked away. *Liar, liar pants*

on fire.

He placed the tray on the nightstand and then sat on the chaise. "Good. I brought you a little something."

Asa pulled upright in the bed, clutching the sheet against her chest. "Thank you. This is the very first time anyone has ever brought me breakfast in bed."

"Well, it's not exactly breakfast."

"It's still special. Thank you." She tried to tamp down the stir of excitement mounting in her stomach by sipping the juice, happy to have something in her hands.

"After my swim, I'll cook you a real breakfast."

"I should cook for you for letting me stay here last night."

"You don't owe me, Asa."

"I know, I know. But I feel like I should do something for you."

His smile widened. "Join me for a swim and we'll call it even."

Asa remained quiet for several moments. He hadn't shaved yet, so the hint of stubble on his jaw gave him a rugged outdoorsy appearance. He looked more desirable this morning than he did last night. He was exactly what she wanted, what she dreamed about when she pictured her perfect man. Asa shook her head, dislodging those thoughts. "If that's all I have to do you're easy to please," she finally replied.

"Not really." He flashed his infamous half smile, his dark eyes twinkled.

"O...kay. I'm not going to take that bait."

"I'm not trying to trick you. I pride myself on always being honest. So if you don't know it by now, let me make it very clear. I want you."

His penetrating stare accentuated his words. A solid mass of lust lodged in her chest, making it hard to breathe. She opened her mouth, then closed it. The words she always wanted to hear poured over her like warm sunshine, heating up the hunger for him that she had all but given up on.

The sheet slid off her breasts and settled around her waist.

"I...but...I—"

"Think about it, Asa." He stood up, exposing another raw shot of his sculptured physique. "Can I take the dog with me? He's growing on me."

"Sure." The word was barely audible.

She watched his tight backside until he disappeared behind the door. Tapping her fingernails against the glass helped settle her racing thoughts. Simeon dropped his casual comment and strolled out the room, leaving her unable to reply with a sensible sentence. Even from ten feet away he made her heart rate accelerate, her palms clammy, and her thoughts jumbled.

Asa climbed out of bed still trembling from his declaration. Now what. She wrapped the sheet around her naked body before sauntering to the French doors. She pushed them open and stepped out on the balcony. The morning warmth promised a hot day ahead. She peered down at the huge pool, the glare from the water was blinding.

Simeon stood on the diving board, his arms stretched above his head. Scruffy sat on the side looking up at him. Simeon swung his arms in circular motions then took two graceful jumps and dived into the water. Asa watched as his lean body pierced the water with hardly a splash. He made it half way to the other side by just flapping his feet.

He'd taken several laps before she ran inside and pulled her skimpiest bikini from her bag.

"I want you too," she whispered.

§ § §

Simeon caught a glimpse of Asa before going in the water. The sheet did little to hide her creamy thighs. His penis jerked against his swim trunks as he broke the plane of water. Maybe the swim would take his mind off of the impossible. She wanted her house. He needed to complete the project. As long as they remained at opposite ends of the spectrum it was useless to pretend they could have anything. He stroked hard against the water until his arms ached.

Minutes later, Asa glided onto patio in a tiny bikini. Her silky skin gleamed in the sunlight. Any relief the water had provided evaporated when she dived in the water and swam toward him. A goddess would be the only way to describe her. He bit his lip to keep from grabbing her as she neared him. Her round butt bobbed on top of the water. Her awkward form did nothing to diminish his

76

excruciating desire for her. His morning swims helped free his thoughts to concentrate on the day's matters. No such luck graced him this morning.

"I'm glad you decided to come in," he said when she lifted her head out of the water.

"You made the water look irresistible. Besides I could use the exercise."

"I'm just about finished, but I'll race you back."

She looked back as if measuring the distance. "Okay. Go." She pushed off.

He eyed her slim legs and butt for a moment before shoving away from the wall and shooting past her. He finished a full length ahead of her.

"I almost beat you." She used her hand to swipe water from her face.

"I'll let you win next time."

"I hope you mean that." She turned over and floated on her back.

Simeon climbed the stairs out of the water. The soreness in his arms and legs made it impossible to swim another lap. He grabbed a towel and dried his hair. "I'll start breakfast so we can meet with the electrician."

"I'll be right in after a few more laps."

Simeon nodded. Coffee might get his brain chugging, because the only thing that seemed important right now was getting Asa into his bed. That tiny piece of material she called a bathing suit didn't help matters. Instead of imagining what lay hidden under her clothes, this morning every curve and contour of her beautiful body was revealed.

By the time she came in the kitchen, breakfast was on the table and the throbbing in his loins had subsided to a slow burn.

"I can't believe I'm saying this but I'm starved. After all I ate last night, I shouldn't eat for a week." Asa sat at the counter.

"A woman with an appetite. I don't think I've ever seen one of those before." He placed toast in front of her.

"Shut up and pass the bacon." She swatted his hand. "I have lots of stuff to do today, so we better get going. My realtor is nice enough to allow me to use his offices." She stuffed bacon into her mouth. "But I can't keep doing that." She talked with her mouth full.

"Slow down, we've got a little time." He sipped his coffee. "You can use offices in my suite for as long as you like. We can give you Internet access, a phone, and my assistant can help you."

Her eyes widened. "Are you serious? That would be fantastic. I can only use my realtor offices for a few hours a day. Are you sure?"

"I am."

She leaned. "Why are you being nice?. I don't get it." over and pecked his cheek.

Before she could pull away he placed his hand behind her neck, found her mouth and kissed her. Her salty tongue tasted wonderful, sinful. Her pulse drummed against his thumb, heightening his sensation.

He released her and peered into her light brown eyes. "I couldn't resist another moment. I hope my behavior or my comment earlier today didn't make you nervous."

She put her fork down. "No, not at all. Surprised, maybe, but not nervous. You're full of surprises."

"How so?"

"You're different. Nothing like I remembered. In high school I don't think I ever saw you smile. Now it seems as if you've found your playful side again. I don't know this side of you."

"There wasn't a whole lot to smile about in high school. Those were rough years for me." He sipped his coffee. Admitting his family's dysfunction wasn't easy. Most days he was able to ignore that period of his life.

"Rough in what way?" she asked.

He put down the coffee cup and searched her face. Was she mocking him? The whole town knew his father would rather drink his paycheck than buy food for his family. They even had a nickname for him, 'boozer the loser'.

"It's getting late. We better get going." *No need to dig up those memories now.*

Chapter Nine

Two days and nothing. No message, not even a call. "Some seduction plan that turned out to be," Asa muttered as she made her way down the stairs.

Her stomach knotted, reminding her of the foolishness for expecting more. Simeon remained an enigma. She needed to give up. He may have wanted her, but something kept him from crossing that line. He had followed her back to her house, watched as the electrician replaced a few blown fuses, and disappeared.

She sat down in an overstuffed chair with her sketch pad. A few more pieces were needed for the fashion show. She drew a sketch of Simeon's broad shoulders and sharp jaw, before crumpling the paper and dropping it on the floor.

There was a small glimmer of hope for the house. Enough for her to stroke and nurture until she could convince him that this house deserved saving. She wrapped her arms around her waist while staring at the water stain on the ceiling. Did every ceiling in this house have some major defect?

"Come on, Scruffy, let's get you outside. I need to get to the bookstore before Dakota starts questioning where we are."

The dog bounced out the door ahead of her. He scurried out of sight behind an unruly forsythia bush without its yellow blossoms. She crept down the stairs after him, mindful of splinters from the rickety banister. The tall, damp grass tickled her ankles. No wonder Simeon wanted to level the block. It looked like nobody cared.

§ § §

"It's about time you showed up." Dakota greeted her when she walked in the store. "I wasn't sure you'd get here before lunch." Dakota held an arm full of books.

"I'm not used to having a dog. It takes extra time getting out of the house in the morning. Then I ran into Mrs. Donald, called someone to cut the grass, spoke to my accountant and my seamstress in New York. I've put in a full day's work and it's only noon," Asa walked behind the counter and perched on the edge of the stool.

Dakota set the books on the counter. She eyed the dog for a moment before patting his head.

"I've got a really good idea," Asa tapped her finger against her cheek.

"Are you going to stop grinning and tell me what it is?"

"I could throw a block party to rally the residents against the strip mall. It could be just like old times."

"How are you going to organize a block party, get the shop ready, and save the house? It's too much."

"I can do it. It wouldn't take much. I could ask all the neighbors to help organize and hire a caterer. Or bring potluck like they used to. Entertainment would be pretty easy, a few games for the kids, some horseshoes, checkers and dominos. Some music." She crossed her leg. "See, I've done it already." She brushed her hands together.

"Asa, in a few months there won't be any houses left

on that block. It's practically deserted already." She stroked her sister's shoulder. "When are you going to accept reality?"

Asa shook her head without meeting her sister's eyes. "Pepa worked hard for that house. We should keep it in the family."

"Are you sure this is about Pepa?" Dakota continued to stroke her sister's arm.

"What do you think it's about?"

"Only you can answer that. But maybe—and this is only my take on the situation, you were married to a jackass so you're feeling deserted, deceived, and deflated. Right now, you're looking for comfort. It's like taking off those awful pointy-toes shoes and putting on your favorite slippers."

Asa spun her back to her sister. "Nope, that's not it."

"I hope you're not getting your hopes up too high, Asa. Even if Simeon decides to leave the house alone, it would take a small fortune to make the place livable. There are new townhouses and condominiums down on the Riverfront. You should take a look at them."

"Money is not the issue. I don't want something without character or to live with a bunch of strangers. I lived with a stranger for two years and it's no fun."

"You'll make new friends."

"Can I use your computer? I want to do a little web-surfing to see what I can find out about Simeon."

"You can use the computer in the office." Dakota

nodded to the back of the store.

"I need to call the realtor that's looking for the studio and contact a few fabric suppliers." Asa jumped up. "This shouldn't take too long."

In the small office Asa typed Simeon's name into the computer. In an instant a list of relevant topics flashed on the screen. She found pictures of him with the mayor and the governor. His broad smile beamed across the page. He'd made the front page of The Weekender as one of the wealthiest eligible bachelors in the tri-state area. There were several magazine articles and news clippings about his philanthropic work. She couldn't find anything on the Golden Leaf Community. Finally, her eyes settled on a feature about the community center across town.

Asa read the story twice. She rubbed her forehead with the heel of her palm. With all those glowing accolades her task to save the house seemed more daunting. His wonderful speech received praise from several elected and government officials. There was even a brief comment from a Golden Leaf resident proclaiming the benefits of all his good works.

"Traitor," Asa shut down the computer.

"Are you going to be much longer?" Dakota stood in the doorway of her office.

Asa groaned and pushed away from the desk.

"Why the long face. Did something bad happen?"

"Nothing I can't handle." Asa squared her shoulders.

"Ooookay," Dakota walked to the front of the store. "Let's go to lunch across the street."

Dakota led the way to the small café. The noise level inside was deafening. Someone called out numbers for orders that were ready for pick-up. And the kitchen staff released their frustration with the heat by slamming the oven door each time they removed a slice of pizza. A thick crowd gathered around the cash register to pay for their lunches.

Dakota pointed to a table in the corner. "Someone is getting up back there. Grab those seats for us, Asa."

Asa gave her sister her lunch order and rushed to the table. She pulled the small table away from the wall to make room for the two of them.

By the time her sister came to the table the crowd had begun to thin and the noise level had dropped.

"It's good to have you back in the city again. I missed our lunches together." Dakota placed the trays on the table.

"I know. Atlanta never felt like home."

"Maybe I should plan a party. You know...invite the cousins so we can sit around and reminisce about the good old days." Dakota pushed her salad around her plate without taking a bite. She put her fork down. "So, any luck finding a place to open your studio?"

"There are two places I like. I'll make a decision soon." Asa finished the last of her salad. "Why aren't you eating?"

Dakota shrugged. "So what's with Simeon?"

Asa hadn't mentioned her overnight stay with Simeon. The last thing she wanted was more teasing. She put her soda can down. "How would I know? One thing for sure I never did get that fancy dinner at the hotel."

"I can take you tonight," Dakota replied. "Let's do it, we'll make it a night."

"Dakota, if it was about the food I could take myself."

"Ohhh, what does that mean? Was it more than dinner?" Dakota leaned forward.

"Never mind."

§ § §

He eyed the phone. He should have called her by now. A quick apology, a little groveling, and setting a date for dinner should be easy. She wanted to keep her house and he wanted her. Mixing the two was a toxic cocktail. Combining business with pleasure never worked out in his favor. But he wanted to do just that. Succumbing to carnal desire almost brought down a president, cost a few mayors their offices, and brought a golfing great to his knees. Simeon needed to be careful. He wouldn't be at peace until Golden Leaf became a strip mall and dad's favorite bench was made into kindling.

But the intense pleasure flowing through his veins could not be denied. He needed more time with Asa. Any hot-bloodied man would.

He picked up the phone and dialed her number.

"I still owe you dinner." He didn't introduce himself.

"Uh, that you do. I thought you were avoiding me."

"Never. Can I pick you up this evening at six?"

There was a long pause. His stomach knotted while he waited for her to reply.

"Tonight?"

"I know it's short notice, but I'd really like to see you." He drummed his fingers on the desk.

"Six is fine. See you then."

He hung up and reared back in his chair. Saving the Conroy home was not an option. Her large dark eyes had begged for understanding. How could he tell her the house was coming down as soon as the ink dried on all the contracts?

He opened his briefcase. The two contracts were on top. He spread them out on the desk. The words blurred into a gray haze.

After dinner tonight he'd tell her the project couldn't be stopped. It would put an end to their relationship before it actually got started. That was always the course for them. But this would be the longest dinner in history. Maybe he'd talk her into his bed, before delivering the bad news.

He picked up the phone and buzzed Catherine.

"Yes." She came into his office with a pad in hand. "I need reservations at the Hotel DuPont tonight."

"Again?" She smirked.

"Tell them I want two Hazelnut Soufflés, but I don't want them to begin the preparation until after we've finished our entrees."

"You hate waiting." She wrote down his instructions. "Tonight must be special." Catherine raised an eyebrow.

Simeon turned to face his computer. "It's been a long time and I have a taste for something decadent."

"Do you need anything else?" Catherine prepared to leave.

"One more thing." He scribbled a note on a piece of paper and handed it to her. "I'll need you to find me one of these and have it wrapped. That'll be it."

She glanced at the note and curled her lip. "Where am I supposed to find one of these? Aren't these things antiques now?"

"Use your magic, you'll find one. I don't care what it costs." She nodded. "Oh, your brother called this morning."

"What did he want?"

"He wouldn't say, and he wouldn't leave a message. Do you want me to get him on the phone?"

If Brian called in the middle of the day it must be important. The Mission kept him so busy they seldom found time to get together. The last time he called he needed new bedding for the cots.

Donating money to his brother's causes made Simeon feel like he was doing something meaningful. If someone had opened a place like that years ago it could have helped their hapless father. Maybe they could have figured out why Nolan Harper found so much happiness at the bottom of a liquor bottle.

"Simeon." Catherine waited till she had his full attention. "You have a meeting with the Operating Committee in a few minutes. They're gathering now in the large conference room. Everything you requested is set up.”

He picked up his folder and stood. “And please call the car service. Tell them to detail my car. Let them know I want it back here by five.”

The Operating Committee owed him an update on the strip mall and the community center. If everything went according to plan, the demolition on Excalibur Avenue could start in a month. And the new community center could be under way in less than a year. Just in time to memorialize the two-year anniversary of his mother’s death. *He had to stop worrying about what Asa would think.*

Chapter Ten

The conference room grew warmer. Simeon glanced at his watch. The meeting needed to come to a close. Nothing would keep him from dinner with Asa. Not even the potential to make more money. He stacked his papers then signaled with his hand to get everyone's attention.

He cleared his throat. "We have to table the remaining agenda items until our next meeting."

"I think we've covered the important details. The funds for front-end loading of the planned community are secure. Delaware Wrecking has our schedule and the demolition date is set. The leases for the strip mall are being prepared. I'll follow-up on the details of the grant and shoot you an e-mail tomorrow," said Brad Stevens as he placed his papers into the folder.

"Fine." Simeon stood up and nodded to the committee. "Brad, I'll need you to run down the questions on the lot size for the center. I don't want any surprises."

"Sure thing." Brad scribbled a note.

When he reached his office, Catherine's clean desk signaled she was gone for the day. He picked up the phone and dialed Asa's number.

"I just want to be sure we're still on."

"Of course. I'm getting ready." The tender sound of her voice ricocheted to his heart, reinforcing his draw for her.

"See you shortly."

He rushed into his Italian marbled en-suite bathroom. After a quick shower, he dressed in a dark suit. The elevator descended to the lobby. He caught a glimpse of his crooked tie in the mirror and made the necessary adjustment.

His Mercedes had been cleaned as requested and gleamed in the designated spot in front of his building. He backed the car out of the parking space. All day he'd played with the words to let Asa know he wouldn't change the project. No matter how he put it, she wouldn't be happy. There was no way to have his project and Asa, too.

He eased the pressure on the accelerator before shifting into the right lane. His heart thumped fast making it difficult to focus on the drive.

The site for the planned community sat just ahead on the right. On schedule, construction was set to begin in a few weeks. His mother didn't smile often, but the day he told her about the project her face lit up like an excited child. He drove by the huge Harper Enterprise sign. Elation bubbled in his stomach.

He cruised several more blocks before turning onto Excalibur Drive. The Conroy house was the only house on the block with the porch lights on. The sun hadn't begun to set, but the street had a picturesque glow.

After shutting off the car he surveyed the block. The quiet street used to be the liveliest in the neighborhood. Tonight it didn't look as intimidating as it when he was a teenager. He shrugged. In a few weeks the whole block would be a pile of rubble.

He stepped out of the car. With his hands shoved in his pockets, he glared up at the house. Asa walked past the upstairs window, her silhouette moved back and forth across the room in a flurry of activity. Then she stood motionless for several seconds. Even in the shadows, he detected her gracefulness; her fluid motion resembled a ballerina. His attraction for her had never diminished, maybe it was stronger.

When she extinguished the light, he reached into the passenger seat and removed the neatly wrapped gift. At the sound of the shrill doorbell, the dog barked.

She opened the door. "I wondered how long you were going to stand outside and stare at the house." Scruffy ran out. After a thorough sniff of Simeon's shoes, he wagged his tail.

Without addressing her question, he drew her into his arms. His body stiffened as he found the warm sweetness of her mouth. Years of longing faded. Her crisp, floral cologne hit his senses with a force to strong for him to resist. He pulled her closer, lifting her feet off the ground.

She released his mouth before he wanted. "Wow, Simeon. I wasn't expecting that."

"What were you expecting?" He looked down at her.

"With you, it's hard to say." She was teasing him and he liked the banter.

"I've been thinking about doing that all day." He grabbed her by the waist, pulled her into his chest and kissed her again. "You look so good, I couldn't help myself." The strapless maxi dress she wore exposed the golden hue of her shoulders. He traced his finger along her collarbone and down her arm. "You saw me from upstairs?" He responded to her original question while his finger lingered on her warm skin.

"I did. Why were you standing there, like that?" She searched his eyes.

"I was falling for your magic."

"You know it's crazy for us to go out when we have such opposing ideas."

"I do it all the time when I'm negotiating with clients."

"Do you kiss them, too?"

He shook his head. "Not usually."

"Then you kissed me to what, to divert my attention away from my goal?"

"Is it working?"

"Nope." She dropped her head. "I remind myself every day of my purpose for moving home and all the things I need to get done." She pulled her pocketbook onto her shoulder.

"I hope I'm on that list and I'd like to get you in my bed, soon."

"I pray you're not getting your hopes up either." She batted her long lashes.

"Touché."

She motioned to Scruffy to go outside.

While they waited on the dog, he handed her the gift.

"What's this?" Her smiled strengthened his resolve. "I didn't know we were doing presents. I don't have anything to give you."

"I wasn't expecting anything. Go ahead, open it."

She ripped the paper off and released a squeal that pierced his ears.

"I don't believe you bought me a CD player!" She turned the shiny red player over in her hands. "It's exactly like the one my father bought me. How could you remember the color and the make? You didn't need to do this."

"Oh, yes, I did. You were right. I broke the first one. I was an angry teenager that adored you and was jealous of you all at the same time. The least I could do was buy you another. I know no one listens to them anymore..."

She rose up on her toes and brushed her soft lips against his cheek. "Thank you very much. I have a few disks I still enjoy. Thank you." Her fingers lingered on his cheek.

"You look stunning as usual. Nice dress." He needed to break the trance before he was swallowed up by his attraction.

"You like it. It's from my collection." She pivoted on her toes. "I'm thinking about including it in my Fashion Week show, but I'm not sure if I like this knit."

"Fashion Week, huh? I'm impressed."

"You should be, buddy." She nudged him before closing the door behind the dog. "I've been trying to get in for several years. This year I finally got my invitation. Do you have any idea what this could lead to?"

"Success," he kissed her forehead.

She accepted his arm and together they walked to the car.

They drove several blocks without talking. He adjusted the music. Taking her to dinner was flirting with fire. He needed to manage an entire meal without giving in to what she wanted. Damn. His loins tightened every time he looked at her.

He pulled into the valet lane of the Hotel DuPont. An attendant rushed to open the door for Asa. "Please leave my car parked here on the street." He motioned to an empty space in front of the hotel before handing the attendant a large bill. With his hand on her back he guided her inside.

§ § §

Asa caught Simeon's eye as he led her across the ornate lobby to the restaurant. A mixture of excitement mingled with trepidation ran down her spine. She could envision Mim's disappoint if she knew instead of fighting to save the house Asa was flirting with the enemy.

Two women seated in the lobby stopped talking and stared as they made their way to the restaurant. One woman pushed her nose in the air when Asa caught her eye. Asa suppressed her grin and gripped Simeon's arm a little tighter.

"Friends of yours?" Asa tilted her head at the women.

Simeon chuckled. "Do you think I know every woman in Delaware?"

"Well, they look like they would like to get to know you. I think the blonde is actually drooling."

He planted a kiss on her cheek and slipped his hand around her waist. "That ought to send her a message, don't you think?"

"Uh huh." Asa fought the blush warming her face. Every kiss pulled her closer to surrendering the resistance she was trying to hold on to. Dealing with the studio, the house, and her feelings for Simeon was almost more than she could manage. But she would. No way could she allow her emotions to derail her plans this time.

The aroma of garlic and butter drifted past her nose. Asa took a deep breath, savoring the rich scent. "Where are we going? The restaurant is that way." Asa pointed beyond the bank of elevators.

"We're having dinner in a private dining room, upstairs. Since I stood you up I thought I would make this dinner a special one."

Asa's legs began to tremble. If he wanted to sweep her off her feet, his plan was working. "I'm impressed."

He gave her a wicked smile. "And you haven't even tasted the meal yet."

She gave his arm a playful slap and then cut her eyes at a young couple in front of them waiting for the elevator. "We'll talk about this later, in private."

The young girl wasn't much older than twenty; her incessant giggles reminded Asa of falling in love, when the relationship was still in that sweet spot, where everything was grand and new. Too bad, relationships didn't stay in that zone forever.

The young couple stepped into the elevator and held the door open for them.

"We'll catch the next car." Simeon waved them on.

Before the doors closed, Simeon leaned close. "Isn't young love refreshing? Don't you wish you were in love like that again?"

"No, thank you, I'll pass," Asa clasped her hands.

"Oh, come on, doesn't every woman want to find true love?"

"Is there such a thing as true love or soul mates? It's all a crock. It's a story men tell us to get to the goodies." She stepped closer to him. "You might as well admit it. I'm onto you."

"Umm, I don't know if I can answer for all men."

"Then answer for yourself." She studied his face, waiting for his reply.

An empty elevator arrived. He guided her in and then stood so close she thought he might hear her heart beating. The attention from him was exciting, but she wouldn't wallow in fairytale land. Not again. He had something she wanted and the minute she forgot her purpose she could lose everything.

He must have read her thoughts. With no preamble he wrapped his arms around her waist and peered into her eyes. "I can't get enough of you. I think I'm becoming addicted." He pressed his mouth to hers.

Her body came alive with his touch. Yielding to the

desire, she pressed her breasts, her stomach, and her thighs against his body. Her brain screamed for her to stop. His hands roamed across her bare shoulders, blazing a steaming trail she didn't want to abandon. His solid body felt like hot steel in her hands.

The bell sounded when the elevator reached the second floor and the doors opened. Instead of releasing her, Simeon continued to weave warm, wet circles around her tongue. Forget dinner, she wanted to move to dessert.

"Excuse me, is this your floor?"

Simeon gave her a final peck before addressing the well-dressed hotel patron. "Yes, it is, sorry if we've delayed you."

Simeon released her, grabbed her hand and led her out of the elevator. She giggled while matching his long strides.

"The private dining room is just down the hall on the right." His voice sounded as giddy as she felt. A small table sat in the middle of the quaint, dimly lit private dining room. A single white tapered candle sat in a crystal holder in the center of the table.

"Very nice," Asa entered the room. The appointments were as elegant as those in the main restaurant.

"I hope this means you forgive me." Simeon held out the chair and gave a gallant bow.

"Yes, I forgave you the first time you asked."

A server materialized from a side door and Simeon stepped away to talk with him.

Asa took a deep breath and exhaled through her mouth. So far, this was the most romantic thing anyone had ever done for her. He could be the right person, but this was the wrong time. She placed her hands in her lap and closed her eyes. Focus.

She didn't have time to get involved with anyone. Certainly not Simeon, they shared too much history—most of which was negative—to forge a serious relationship. His numerous rejections still scorched her ego. The next man in her life needed to show interest in her from the day they met.

Simeon was sophisticated and handsome as hell; but she did not intend to fall for that again. Fashion week was in a few months. She needed to focus on the final pieces. Chaos best described the state of her studio plans and the house. Keeping her focus on all of that should be enough to help her ignore his charm. But it wasn't.

Simeon returned to the table and slid his chair closer. "So you're not interested in settling down and finding true love?" His velvety voice scrambled her thoughts. He had to be trying to knock her off her game.

She examined his face. "Are we still on that conversation? No, right now I'm not thinking about any of that."

His eyes widened. "Is that right?"

Asa rested her chin in her palm and peered into his eyes. Something twinkled in the dark pools. "Are you looking?"

"No. No I'm not."

"Why not? Too busy enjoying your bachelor status?" She wanted to take the attention off her.

"There's that sharp wit again." He laughed. "No, my business keeps me pretty busy. I don't have the time to devote to a serious relationship."

"Surely, there is no shortage of women that would like nothing better than to tie you down on your terms."

"I haven't found the right woman yet."

"Are you looking, or do you expect her to fall in your lap?"

Simeon reached for her hand. "When she falls into my lap, you better believe I'll never let go."

His baritone voice sounded convincing, but a man with everything going for him wasn't single unless there was a glitch. Something must be wrong with him.

Asa swallowed hard. "Interesting. You sound convincing."

"So, tell me, what went wrong with your marriage." Asa shifted in her seat. Her hand trembled when she reached for the water goblet. Should she tell him the truth or give him the rehearsed version? She wanted to be honest.

"In the beginning things seemed wonderful, but maybe we were too young or maybe marriage wasn't as exciting as he thought it was going to be. After two years he found more fun in anything and everything but me. He'd rather watch paint dry than spend an evening at home."

"Ouch." Simeon winced. "The man was crazy. What

could be more exciting than you?"

"Well, let's see; Yvonne, Marcy, Stacy, and a little redhead named Rebecca."

"If this is difficult you don't have to talk about it."

"No...no, I don't mind. I've moved on." She paused for several moments. "I haven't told my sisters all this yet. I blamed myself. My parents didn't want me to get married. They wanted me to wait. But you know...youth, love, and all that stuff made a dangerous combination. I thought marriage would make me happy, improve my life." She relaxed her shoulders, the tension eased.

"What was wrong with your life? Why did it need improving?"

She shrugged. "Something was missing." Asa looked beyond Simeon at the gold flecked wallpaper.

"Did your parents know your marriage was in trouble?"

She dropped her gaze. "No, I tried to make it work. I never told them. My parents came for a visit the year before they died. I think my mother could see the stress in our relationship. She asked lots of questions." Asa picked up the salt and pepper shakers and set them back down. "I remember the big cheesy smile I gave her when I told her Eric and I were doing just fine. I was belligerent, accusing her of wanting my marriage to fail when she continued to ask questions. Eric couldn't even fake it for the week my parents visited. On their last night in town he didn't even come home." Asa ran her hand over the tablecloth. "I could see disappointment in my mother's eyes, but she never said anything."

Simeon covered her hand with his. "I'm sure your mother wanted the best for you."

"Let's talk about something more upbeat. That time is behind me. I want to forget it."

"Fine. Then why don't you tell me what's on your mind tonight?" He added, "As if I don't already know."

Before she could respond, the server showed up. Simeon ordered a bottle of Cabernet Sauvignon. When the server walked away, Simeon folded his hands on the table and stared at Asa, waiting on her reply.

"We talked a little bit the other night about the house. I hope you've given it some thought. Maybe we can come up with ideas so the house doesn't get torn down."

He opened his mouth and closed it again. He released her hand and laid his palms on the table. "Asa, I know you want to save the house. I really don't think there's anything I can do at this stage to divert or change the project." He spoke slow and measured. "The neighborhood needs access to affordable goods."

"By tearing down the houses? Then there won't even be a neighborhood."

"This project will do a lot of good for a lot of people. It will create jobs."

"Not everyone thinks it's such a good idea," Asa countered.

"Before we approached any investors we did our research. We performed several surveys. Your sister, Melissa gave us the okay. Neither of your sisters raised any objections at the time. Why is this becoming a major issue this late in the game?"

Their server cleared his throat and asked if they were ready to order dinner. Asa accepted the menu. She stared at the words until they blurred. Maybe if she had been straight with her sisters about leaving Atlanta and opening a shop in Delaware everything would have turned out differently.

The server listened to their dinner request without jotting down any notes. Afterward he nodded and walked away.

Asa sipped her wine, happy to take a moment to gather her thoughts. Simeon gazed at her over his glass. She would lose the battle for her house and for his love. The urge to flee swept over her.

That first night when he stepped on her porch, he tugged at her heart. Since then an inferno seized her. She was still in love with him. Pretending anything else was useless. She dropped her eyes, picked up the pepper shaker and moved it across the table.

"There's nothing I can do. If our due diligence turns up nothing, we have to move forward." He held his hands in midair.

"What if I wasn't the only one that wanted that block left alone?"

"It wouldn't matter."

Moving back to Bristol was the right thing to do. Even without the house, living here made her happy and, content. She wouldn't run away.

The server returned with their dinner. Simeon's rib-eye

steak sizzled in butter on his plate and the aroma of her seared sea bass made her mouth water. Without replying to Simeon's comment, she tasted a piece of the flaky fish. Instead of talking about the house they chatted about some of their classmates. If she couldn't work with Simeon to save the house, then she would work around him.

"The other day you offered me use of an office in your suite. Is it still available?"

"It's all set up. All you have to do is show up." He placed his knife and fork across the plate.

"I'll be there tomorrow."

"I'm looking forward to having you around."

She suppressed the pang of excitement, his words stirred in her stomach.

After their plates were removed from the table, Asa surveyed his face. The dimples that showed up when he smiled and the high cheekbones make him even more handsome. Too bad they couldn't seize the opportunity years ago when they had the chance.

"Why didn't you like me in high school, Simeon?" She hadn't planned to ask that question, but now she needed to know. Was her timing with men always off? Did Simeon have a reason for ignoring her; ditching her hopes even before they were fully formed?

Shock registered in his eyes. "Err...I...I..." he muttered.

"It's not a hard question. You had to know I had a crush on you. I followed you around like a lovesick puppy. No matter how hard I tried to get your attention you ignored me. I just want to know why."

"I didn't know that...I was always trying to..." He reached for his wine and took a long swallow. "You were the girl that lived on the right side of the tracks. I lived on the wrong side. Girls like you didn't date guys like me."

Asa laughed at his reply. "What are you talking about? You're kidding me, right?" She continued to laugh.

He looked at her and shook his head. "We were the poor family. My father made us the laughing stock of the city. Everyone knew Nolan Harper, the town drunk, and his tattered family."

She stopped laughing and stared at him. Could he be serious? "We were all poor. I didn't look down on you. You were the cutest guy in school. You were smart and so serious. Unlike the other guys in our class, you had a solidness about you that I liked. Besides, no one could have been poorer than my family."

He cleared his throat and looked away. "It doesn't matter." He removed his napkin from his lap, folded it into a neat rectangle and placed it on the table. "I think it's time I take you home."

"Wait a minute." Her eyes widened. "What about my house?"

"I think I know what you want." He stood up. "I told you I can't make any promises."

"Have you at least thought about other options?"

"I have. Give me a few weeks." He reached for her hand to help her up.

"Do I have a few weeks?"

"You do if I say you do." *Because this time I'm in control.*

Chapter Eleven

Asa punched her pillow and turned over. It was too early to get up; she needed a few more hours of sleep. She wasn't used to crawling into bed after three, but at least she'd finished cutting and pinning the asymmetrical jacket. The ruffled shawl collar would be an instant hit.

She turned on her back and opened her eyes. The morning sun streamed through the opened curtains, blanketing the room with blinding light. When Simeon kissed her good night, pressing his leg between her thighs, she almost invited him to spend the night. Lust gnawed at her willpower. Every time Simeon looked at her she wanted to open her arms and grant him his wish.

It was time to move to Plan B.

The lollipop ringtone from her cell phone shook her from daydreaming about Simeon. Instead she scrambled to find her ringing cell phone. She patted the bed with wild random swats. It was somewhere here.

What crazy person would have the audacity to call this early in the morning? Scruffy gave her a slow yawn as she smacked the bed. She found it buried under the top sheet.

Eric's number appeared on the display. She contemplated accepting his call.

"Yes Eric, what do you want?"

"I've been calling you. Why haven't you answered?"

"I thought after a while you'd get the message." Her voice was terse, maybe that would shoo him away.

"Well, huh. You didn't respond to the e-mails I sent

either, so I decided to keep calling." He paused. "I went past the condo the other day. They said you moved."

Asa hesitated, not certain she wanted him to know where she'd gone. Eric never wanted to come to Delaware to visit her family. He made excuses why they couldn't make the trip; it was too far, or too cold. She wasn't worried that he would come to Delaware now. "I've moved."

"Oh, I see. And you weren't going to tell me?"

"We're divorced, Eric, I don't have to report in to you anymore."

"You're right, you're right. My bad. I didn't mean to pry. I only wanted to check on you. You know I still care about you."

"I'm fine. Look, I've got to go."

"So where are you? Maybe I'll stop by and see you some time."

"I don't think that's a good idea. Besides, I moved back home."

"Why the hell did you move all the way back up there? That's pure stupidity. To go running back home like a baby." His anger pierced the phone. "When are you going to stop worrying about what your family thinks about you?"

"Eric, don't call me anymore. We're done."

"We'll see about that. We'll be done when I say so. I still love you and there isn't a piece of paper that can shut off my feelings."

Asa swallowed. She didn't miss arguing with him. She didn't miss the way he made her feel small and insignificant. And she didn't miss him. Why he continued to call remained a mystery. His latest ladylove probably just dumped him and he wanted to return to something familiar. But she wasn't that naïve girl she used to be.

"Bye, Eric." She disconnected the call and dropped her head back on the pillow. "How long am I going to feel so crappy?"

The dog responded by nuzzling his head against her hand until she rubbed his chin. She contemplated the ceiling. A fresh coat of paint could hide that huge water stain. One afternoon and a little hard work would make this room happy again. She'd have to add that to her growing list.

She turned on her side. Last night's dinner made her frown.

Nothing was accomplished. Last night put her no closer to proving to her family she didn't always screw up. Sitting across the table from Simeon had fulfilled one of her fantasies, a date with her first crush, but nothing more. His charm nearly made her forget the purpose for the evening. Now it was time to step off the cloud and face reality.

They left the hotel before the pastry chef even served the special desert. The look that clouded Simeon's eyes needled her. Growing up she never viewed Bristol as a place with a right side or wrong side of the tracks. Did he really mean that comment or was he trying to distract her?

The dog licked his right paw at the edge of the bed. He

stopped for a moment to sniff her then resumed his task. She patted him on the head, enjoying the warm feel of his soft coat. Why couldn't her love life provide the same kind of quiet contentment?

Scruffy yelped, giving her hand another stiff shove before jumping from the bed. At the door he spun around, his tail brushing the doorframe. She climbed out of bed and followed him downstairs.

Asa opened the kitchen door for him to go out. He meandered about the yard, sniffing his way from one bush to the next. She put a cup of water in the microwave. Tea helped her to think straight. Did she only imagine the sparkle in Simeon's eyes as he led her to the private dining room? Why did she feel so exhilarated whenever he came near her or touched her?

She dialed Dakota. "Can you pop in and watch the dog for me today? I'm going to be tied up most of the day."

"No problem. I'll pick him up and bring him here."

"Are you available for dinner tonight? My treat." Asa put sugar in her tea.

"No. I'm…I'm…"

"If you don't want to tell me, I understand."

"I have plans tonight. A date of sorts." Dakota was hesitant.

After the normal small talk they ended the call. From the kitchen, she watched the dog bury his nose in the tall grass. With her arms crossed over her chest, she leaned against the counter and waited for the microwave to beep.

Simeon didn't have anyone special in his life and neither did she. Maybe, just maybe... She shook her head, forcing those thoughts out. But the kisses still lingered on her lips and promised to keep her energized for a few days. Their dinner was a business meeting, a meeting that didn't produce the results she wanted. From now on she would remain focused. The house needed her attention.

She dipped her teabag in the hot liquid and watched the water turn burgundy. Then she dropped in five teaspoons of sugar. The heat from the cup warmed her hands. She let the dog in and headed upstairs.

From the bedroom closet she pulled on a short skirt and a ruffled top. She slipped on a pair of platform sandals. "You be a good boy while I'm gone, okay, Scruffy." She patted the dog on the head before leaving. She backed the car out of the driveway. At a stop light she smacked the dashboard when the car threatened to cut out.

"Come, on baby, don't stop on me now," she whispered as she pulled slowly through the intersection. The car wheezed and began to slow down. She pressed the accelerator to the floor. The car didn't pick up speed. Several more pumps on the accelerator produced nothing. She steered the slow moving car toward the curb.

"I suppose that's as far as we're going for now." She got out and stomped her foot. Lifting the hood could have been useful for someone that understood cars. She knew nothing about cars so why pretend now? Instead, she kicked the tire.

"Having trouble?" A tall man approached. He wore a familiar smile. Asa wondered if she should know him.

"This is an old car and I'm not surprised it conked out. It's been threatening to do this for quite some time."

"I'm Brian. I run the mission." He nodded to the stucco building behind him. "I don't know much about cars, but let me get one of the guys from inside. I've got a good guy that knows a lot about them."

"Brian, I'm Asa. Thank you, but I don't want to keep you from what you were doing."

"It's no trouble. The men here want to be helpful. Let me get him." Brian walked back inside.

She caught her breath when after a few minutes, Simeon walked out of the stucco building.

"Asa, what's wrong, what are you doing here?" His dark eyes flickered with concern as he scanned her from head to toe.

"The gentleman that runs the mission just went inside to get me some help with the car. Why are you here?"

Simeon chuckled. "That gentleman is my brother, Brian. While they look at the car, can I give you a lift somewhere?"

"I was on my way to your office." She pulled her bag out of the back seat and hoisted it onto her shoulder.

"Your car will be in good hands here. I assure you."

Brian came out with a burly man close behind him.

"Well it's not running, so I can't imagine anyone is going to hijack it." Asa handed the key to Simeon's brother.

"I'm parked in back."

She followed Simeon behind the building and slid into the passenger seat when he opened the car door. She raised her sunglasses and peered at him. "You're sure I'm not keeping you from something? You always seems to be rushing from one thing to the next."

"Is that comment in reference to me cutting our dinner short last night?"

"In part, yes. But you seem to be too busy for your own life."

He pulled into traffic. "I have plenty to do, but you're a pleasant distraction."

"I figured talking about your family is a sensitive subject."

"I don't like visiting the past."

"We both have something in our past that we'd like to forget." She turned to him. "Anyway, I enjoyed dinner, too."

"Even though it didn't turn out the way you wanted?"

"The food tasted fantastic. The company was good. I've learned to take pleasure in whatever form it comes."

"Then maybe we can do it again. Come to my house tonight and I'll cook for you."

"Simeon, I don't know. I've got a lot--"

"Oh, come on. I'm a good cook. You can bring your four legged friend, too."

"You don't cook, you'll probably have your housekeeper prepare a meal," she said.

“No, I’m doing it all.”

She hesitated for a moment, while running her finger along the leather strap of her bag.

He pulled into the parking garage, turned off the car and faced her. “How about it?”

She nodded.

It was too late to back away now.

Chapter Twelve

Simeon watched his assistant walk Asa to the office he had set up for her. His breathing accelerated with each sway of her hips. He shook his head and nearly careened into a woman on his way to his office.

Spending time with Asa might not be one of his best ideas. But he couldn't resist asking her out again. Her bubbly personality drew him in like waves crashing to shore, and if he wasn't careful he'd end up crashing too. As long as her charm didn't derail his project, there was no need to worry.

He dislodged his thoughts of Asa's shapely butt. After tonight, maybe he needed a few days away to get beyond his growing obsession. A trip to the beach to focus on something other than her soft skin, curly dark hair, or radiant smile should help. But first he had to get through tonight without being tripped up by something like stupid emotions.

Dinner with Asa. His house. Tonight. He felt like a million dollar lottery winner. Fate finally smiled down on him. Maybe the Harper curse was broken or maybe he wasn't damned forever, at least not tonight.

Usually he looked forward to matching wits with an opponent. Inviting trouble into his life was normal. Harpers had danced with danger their whole lives. Just being a Harper came with its share of challenges. It prepared him for greater obstacles.

He sunk all of his savings into a development company

with no expertise in construction. After eating beans that first year while he reorganized the business, it got a little easier. His first project, the multiplex, turned out successful after a steep learning curve and several stumbles. But it seemed like eons ago now.

"Are there any messages?" He asked Catherine when she returned.

"Yes, George from the Plaid Group called. He said it was urgent and they want you to call back this afternoon."

"What's it about...the planned community project?"

"He didn't leave a message. Shall I get him on the line now?"

"No, I'll call him back. Is there anything else?"

She rattled off a few more messages. All of them could wait until tomorrow.

"Please call Munson's, have them deliver two large bone-in rib-eyes. And get some fresh seafood too. Lobsters would be nice. And order two large baking potatoes and fresh asparagus."

"Okay, got it. Anything else?"

"Yes, order something sweet for dessert. Have it all delivered to the house around seven tonight. Thanks."

He hurried into his office, lifted the phone receiver and punched in the numbers for The Plaid Group. He knew it without having to look it up.

"George, this is Simeon Harper. You were trying to get in touch with me?"

"Yes, Simeon. Good news. We have all the signatures.

Barring any unforeseen incidents the funds should be released by the end of the week. You can start calling in the heavy equipment. I wanted to stop by your office today to get your signature."

"I'll have Catherine call your assistant to get those documents couriered to me at home. I'll get them back to you tomorrow."

"Sounds good. Let's get this project moving. We've been waiting long enough." There was laughter in George's voice.

"I agree, George. Let's get it done. But I'm looking into an issue regarding the lot size. I expect it will be easy to resolve."

"You're the expert. I'll leave it up to you," George replied before hanging up.

For the last three weeks, he had anticipated final approval. Now that his investors were on board, he didn't have to write any more company checks. There was no turning back now. Both of his projects were set to begin.

The Golden Leaf strip mall for him. The planned community for his mother as promised.

When the opportunity came to buy the fledgling company, she'd assured him he could make it a successful business.

His mother saw the need for the community center and housing from the beginning, calling it one of his best projects. When Nolan Harper died from exposure, they lost their apartment. After living on the streets for two weeks, until space opened in the shelter, he knew he had to do everything he could to help his family pull the Harper name out of the gutter.

He spun his chair around to the window and stared at the traffic below. Everything he ever wanted was within his reach. He took a deep breath.

Asa was having dinner with him in a few hours. When she accepted the invitation her eyes overflowed with hope. He winced at the thought of the pain he would inflict on her. Could they get through the evening without talking about the project?

§ § §

The morning was productive. Fabric samples were ordered. The venue design was set and her realtor was lining up studio properties. She put her pen down and sat back. The satisfaction felt good. Everything seemed to be coming together, except one big booby trap just waiting on her.

In her mind caution signs lit up at the thought of Simeon. But the warnings came too late to heed. Why couldn't they get their timing right? In high school their immature clumsiness kept them apart, now they had managed to find more obstacles to place in their path. Dating Simeon wasn't a smart move. He could crush her world by signing his name on the dotted line. But she couldn't stop, and the betrayal was eating away at her insides.

"Are you ready to call it a day?"

Even before she saw his face, she recognized his deep,

velvet voice. Simeon towered in the office doorway.

"Simeon." Her mouth was dry. She would never grow tired of looking at him. He took the seat in front of the desk and placed his briefcase on the floor. The last couple of days with him had been fantastic.

"I've got an important date tonight, so I can't be late." His mischievous smile made her chuckle.

"Ah, so it's a date now, is it?"

"It is for me." He stood up. "Ready?"

She gathered her things and walked ahead of him to the elevators.

"Did you get much done today?"

"Yes, thanks to you. For starters, I was able to do phone interviews with two designers and I had a virtual tour of a property for the studio. I even convinced Dakota to take care of my dog since I'm going to be getting in late."

Her sister's warning about getting involved with him gnawed at her, but tonight she planned to enjoy dinner.

And nothing more

Chapter Thirteen

Guilt rippled along her spine while she waited for him to change and come back downstairs. Was she fighting hard enough to save the house? Was she betraying her grandparents or parents or even worse, herself?

He prepared dinner with the efficiency of an Iron Chef. Everything she thought she knew about him evaporated as he marinated the steaks and butterflied the lobster tails. Any remembrances of the brooding teenager faded away with the genuine happiness on his face.

Simeon had all the traits of a perfect man. There was just one thing standing between them and even though she could name the mountain, she knew scaling it seemed insurmountable.

"Thanks for inviting me over. You've saved me from another evening of frozen TV dinners and television."

"Is that the only reason you came?"

He led her through the enormous sun-filled kitchen to another large room equipped for entertaining. A leather sectional sat in front of a huge plasma screen TV. Soft music filtered through the air. Brazilian walnut hardwood floors gleamed throughout the first floor. The grandeur of his house made her fight seem foolish. She was trying to save a dump and he was living in a mini-mansion. But his house couldn't have as many memories or treasured moments as hers. Everything here screamed new, with no sentimental value.

"You never answer my questions. Are you only here so you won't have to eat a frozen dinner?"

"That didn't come out quite right, did it? I'm here because while you're being nice to me, I need to enjoy it. No one knows how long it will last."

"That doesn't sound a whole lot better. You make me sound like an ogre."

"Like Mim used to say, 'If the shoe fits, wear it'."

"Did your Mim have a lot of sayings?"

"She had one for every occasion." Asa smiled.

"I think I would have liked your grandmother."

Asa took a seat on the plush sofa and pursed her lips.

"I wasn't that bad in high school. Was I?"

"Worse. I'm not just talking about high school. You terrorized me in grade school, avoided me in high school, and now you're trying to tear down my house."

"Can we call a truce for tonight?" His voice took on that lusty quality, melting her resolve.

The smooth, soulful sound of Raphael Saadiq filled the room. He sang about unrequited love that stroked her heart.

"Asa, did you hear me? Are we calling a truce tonight?"

She shook herself back to reality. "Yes. Tonight let's just enjoy ourselves. How about that?"

"Good. Let me pour you a glass of champagne."

"You're in a good mood tonight." Asa accepted the glass he handed her. She watched as he took a long swallow.

His eyes clouded a moment before he replied, "Yes, I got some good news today, so I'm happy."

"Care to share?" she asked.

His jaw tightened before he shook his head. "It's only work. Tonight, I won't talk about work if you promise not to talk about my project or your house."

She studied him, stunned.

He stared at her for several moments before he added, "Even busy people find time to enjoy a good cooked meal before talking business."

"Mmm hmm." She shifted in her seat. "Okay, no business talk tonight" Since he wanted to nix all conversations relating to business, he'd given her the perfect excuse for not mentioning the rally.

"You have a beautiful home." Asa surveyed the area she could see from where she sat. Elegent detailing was apparent, from the wainscoting to the handcrafted built-ins along with the theater system. Even the media room where they sat could appear on the cover of House Beautiful. No personal touches adorned the room, though. No pictures or mementos, nothing bearing Simeon's personal stamp. It lacked warmth. They could have been sitting in a museum. "I didn't see much of it the last time I was here."

He drained his glass then stood up. "Let me show you around."

"Who did your decorating?"

"Well, my mother planned to help me, but she got sick before we could finish. So, I ended up using a decorator. Someone we found in New York. I don't think she really understood me, so eventually I'll make some changes."

The long mahogany dining table could seat twelve, but only two settings were in place tonight. Two crystal chandeliers hung low over the table. "This room is gorgeous. Is it your favorite?" Asa ran her finger along the table.

"I don't have a favorite."

"There's no room in this huge house that you love to sit in and relax?"

"No. I don't do a lot of sitting." He shrugged. "All these rooms are pretty much the same to me."

"What a pity. My favorite room is my grandparent's bedroom. I remember me and my sisters crawling into their bed on Saturday mornings and begging my grandfather to make pancakes."

He glanced over his shoulder at her, but didn't reply.

Asa's eyes traveled down his long, lean frame. He wore a pair of vintage jeans with a simple T-shirt, quite different from the suit and tie from earlier today. He pointed to the formal living room without stopping and led her down the hall. Asa noticed the stacks of magazines and papers on his desk as he gestured into his office. She slowed her pace and lingered in the only room in the house that looked lived-in. A few framed pictures crammed in the corner of the cluttered desk seemed strategically placed.

There weren't any mismatched pieces of furniture or personal items strewn about like the chaos she enjoyed at home.

"Okay, Simeon, you have to tell me, is your house

always so neat or did you make it picture perfect for me?"

"What...what do you mean?"

"Oh, come on, this isn't a house, it's a museum. The only room that looks lived in is your office."

"I work long hours. I'm not as emotionally tied to this place as you seem to be to yours. I've learned not to grow too attached to anything or anyone."

"I work a lot also. You can see pieces of fabric, sketches, or buttons all over my house."

"When I'm here, most of my time is spent in the office."

"Why do you have a house like this if you have no intention of living in it or enjoying it?"

He looked away. "This house in an investment. Right now I'm only interested in building my business. I'm a man on a mission. Everything else is secondary." He led her back to the kitchen.

Asa watched him pull two lobster tails from the refrigerator and drizzle butter over them before placing them under the broiler. "Tell me what you do in the little bit of time when you're not working?"

He rubbed his chin. "Let's see. I'm trying to remember the last time I wasn't working."

He placed two steaks on the hot, built-in grill.

"I have a place down at the beach that I try to get to several times a year, but it's been months since I was last there." He poured another glass of wine.

For several seconds the only sound came from the

sizzling meat and the crackling sound of the butter. He motioned to refill her glass.

She held up her hand. "No, I better save my next drink for dinner."

He stared at her across the kitchen counter. His dark eyes fixed on her face.

"Why are you looking at me like that?" she asked.

He shook his head. For a brief moment he saw his teenage love. "I guess I'm amazed at how little you've changed. Your hair is almost the same. I used to sit behind you in algebra class and stare at your hair all period. Now, I know why I almost failed that class."

"You did not." Asa laughed.

"Did too." He mimicked her.

"I'm surprised you didn't move away after graduation. Why did you stay?"

"My family is here. I didn't want to leave my mother alone. She had enough hardship to deal with. What about you? Why Delaware and not New York?"

"I thought about New York, but after being in Atlanta, I knew I needed to be closer to my sister."

"Come, let's eat. Dinner is ready."

He carried two plates laden with food into the dimly lit dining room. "I'll be right back." He dashed into the kitchen and returned with a platter containing the lobster tails. A bottle of wine were tucked under each arm.

"This is too much food. How much do you think I eat?"

"I wasn't sure so I tried to cover all the bases. We don't have to eat it all."

Asa couldn't stop grinning. Simeon paid attention to everything she said. He stared at her like she was dessert. Other than his comment about his business, the evening received a pretty high score. Nobody had ever put so much energy into making sure she enjoyed an evening. Simeon had done it twice.

Just relax and have a good time. You're entitled. She bottled up his earlier comment about his focus on work. Her work was first in her life too.

"You said you could have another glass of wine with dinner. I didn't know if you wanted white or red, so I brought both." He held them out for her to choose.

"Let's have the Riesling."

"Good choice." He removed the cork. Her body tingled from the sultry look he gave her.

§ § §

Simeon finished his wine. Half empty platters cluttered the table. Tonight something was different. The reserved partition that seemed to exist between them had disappeared. She looked incredible. He still wanted her, maybe even more than before. He reached for her hand and held it.

"Did you save room for dessert?"

"I always have room for something sweet."

Her brilliant smile stroked his heart. The flickering

candlelight glowed against her skin. He traced her jaw line with his finger. She released a soft moan.

"You are a beautiful woman, has anyone ever told you that?"

She smiled without replying.

He pushed away from the table. "Let me get the fruit." He hurried from the room.

In the kitchen, he braced himself against the granite counter, his fingers straining to absorb the tension in his body. "Get it together man," he whispered. "Now is not the time or place to get tripped up by Asa." His body betrayed him. He grabbed the tray of fruit off the counter. He closed his eyes and took a breath, before going back into the dining room.

"Let's go back in the family room. Grab that wine, will you?" He used his chin to point to the half-empty bottle.

Her skirt rode up as she reached across the table. His eyes traveled the rich creaminess of her skin along her shapely legs and lean thighs and ended with a partial view of her butt. His body jerked to attention.

"Can you get it?" he uttered before averting his eyes.

"Got it," she said. "I'll grab our glasses, too." She followed him out of the dining room.

He placed the tray on the coffee table and then sat next to her.

"I could get used to this treatment." She accepted the fruit. "You do this kind of thing for all your lady friends?"

"There aren't as many lady friends as you think."

"I saw them lining up to talk with you the other night."

"I'm not foolish enough to think that was about me. It's more about the peripherals that come along for the ride."

"Wow, that doesn't sound—"

He held up his hand to stop her. "I'm used to it. It's no big deal."

"Between the two of us we have some pretty crappy personal relationships, don't we?"

"It depends on how you look at it. I'm not looking for anything right now, so for me it's not as crappy."

"If my future were more certain, maybe I'd feel differently." Her voice sounded dreamlike. "The fashion show and the studio keep me busy. So, I'm managing pretty well. Sometime in the future, I want a relationship. I want the whole thing, the house, picket fence and two point five children. I already have the dog."

He nodded. "I don't think the family scenario is for me." He placed a strawberry in her mouth.

"You want to be alone forever?"

He thought for a moment. "Just because you're in a relationship doesn't mean you won't be alone."

She nodded. "No one knows that better than me."

"I've had a little experience in that arena, too. My mother was married for twenty years and most of that time she spent alone."

"I'm sorry to hear that." She gave him a long look.

"Don't be, that's in the past."

Asa looked at her watch. He'd plied her with food and good conversation, but beyond that he had no more tricks to make her stay longer.

"I better get home and check on my dog. I'm not sure how long Dakota is keeping him. If I leave him too long, he gets distressed." She uncrossed her legs and Simeon gazed at her sculpted calves. "I had a nice time. You're a very good cook." She bent down to pick up her purse and he stared openly at her thighs and butt.

He couldn't resist the temptation to taste her. He stood and caressed the smooth, soft skin at the back of her neck. She melted into him as he pressed his lips against hers. He lowered his arms and pulled her closer. Asking her to stay would be foolish.

§ § §

The intensity of her emotions for him burned just as hot as they had years ago. She pressed her body against him. A song played in her head, but she couldn't make out the lyrics. The staccato rhythm thumped along with the beat of her heart.

He lifted her a few inches off the floor while his tongue continued to stroke hers. Her skirt rose up her thighs. His fingers trailed along her back and her flesh tingled. He withdrew his tongue but continued to hold her.

She stared into his eyes. Her mind said release him, but her arms were slow to obey.

His strong hand grazed her back, scorching her skin through the thin cotton of her top. She pressed into his massive steel chest, trying to absorb years of desire in the fever pitch of her heartbeat. He ran his thumb along her jaw, then down the hollow of her neck. She couldn't turn back. Every sense screamed out for him, begging for more. The heat building between them over the last few days couldn't be denied.

He pinned her against the wall, pushed her legs apart, and kissed her again. Deeper this time. His erection throbbed against her. Forgetting her priorities would lead to trouble, the tightening in her stomach confirmed her fears. But the feel of Simeon in her arms smothered her logic. She ran her fingers under his shirt, kneading the corded muscles on his back. The guttural noise that he emitted sounded like her name, mixed with foreplay, and desire. It was enough to make her surrender.

He nibbled her earlobe, capturing it between his teeth. The heat from his mouth cascaded over her shoulder, drowning her with longing so intense it scorched. "I want you, Asa. Tonight. Now."

"Yes, Simeon. Now."

He lifted her top over her head, then pulled her skirt down her legs. He steadied her with his arm as she stepped free of the garment. He inhaled, then gripped her left breast in his large hand, kneading it with a tenderness reserved for infants. His hands moved in agonizing slowness, while her body hungered for him.

She freed his brawny chest, sending several buttons on his shirt skidding across the hardwood floor. She tugged the shirt off and ran her hands over his thick pectoral muscles. The warmth from his body seared her hands.

He felt exactly the way she had imagined, tough, strong, and more masculine than any man she'd ever known. He lowered his head to the nape of her neck. His breath dusted her shoulder as he trailed kisses along the column of her neck and over the curve of her shoulders. When he kissed her his tongue erased all the years of calluses left behind from her marriage. Simeon's essence was etched on every fiber of her being. This was a dangerous place to tread, but she couldn't turn back.

He removed the rest of his clothing and stood before her. In the dim light his body called to her. She folded her fingers around his erection. It throbbed in her hands, causing her core to ache.

"Simeon." Her throaty whisper sounded foreign to her ears.

He lifted her off the floor. She wrapped her arms around his neck then sought his tongue. His response was immediate, providing the assiduous assault she needed. He inserted his finger into her moist core, stoking the fire that he ignited with that first kiss. She released his tongue and buried her head against his neck. Unable to suppress the unintelligible words that rushed through her brain she bit softly into his shoulder.

He massaged her nub. The pressure between her legs mounted, building momentum with each flick of his finger. The intensity of his touch left her breathless. Ecstasy rolled over her like warm heat. She threw her head back and yelled his name as the orgasm jerked her like a marionette.

§ § §

He waited until she finished shaking. He enjoyed every contraction that ripped through her body. Then he carried her into the solarium and laid her on the couch.

"Let me get a condom," he whispered in her ear.

"Hurry." Her husky murmur fueled his desire.

He was gone for only an instant. His heartbeat accelerated when he returned and caught a glimpse of her slender body stretched across the sofa. Her eyes were closed and her hand played between her thighs. He watched with delight as her finger disappeared.

"Let me do that for you." He crawled beside her.

She removed the silver packet from his hand. Her eyes blazed into him as she ripped it open with her teeth. She fit the tip of the latex over the head of his member, taking her time, tantalizing him with payback. He thrust his hips forward to hurry her, but she refused to rush.

"Let me do it." He reached for the condom, but she pushed his hand away.

"I've got this." She continued rolling it to the base of his penis.

"And I've got this." He straddled her as soon as she finished, burying his head in her curls and his shaft deep inside her simultaneously.

Her moist folds gripped his shaft and a paralyzing pleasure ricocheted through his body. All the tortured teenage wet dreams vanished.

Finally.

He planted several kisses along her collarbone then suckled her earlobe. She released a moan laced with pleasure that sent him deeper into her. The moment should have lasted forever, but the mounting pleasure coursing through his loins couldn't be restrained. Beneath him Asa panted and bucked her hips like a wild filly. She wrapped her long legs around his waist, hoisting her hips higher, allowing him greater access.

"Simeon," she sang his name. "I'm coming. Again."

He couldn't hold back another second, her walls locked him in a grip, sending his seed spilling into the constraints of the latex. The spasms ripped through him, draining every muscle in his body. He collapsed on Asa for a moment before rolling his weight off to the side.

She had him, where she wanted him now.

Chapter Fourteen

Carrying her light frame up the stairs was intoxicating. She held on to him with a tight grip around his neck.

"I'm not going to drop you." He whispered in her ear.

"That's the least of my worries," she cooed. "I just don't want to let you go."

"I'm not going anywhere. And neither are you." He placed her on his bed. Her gorgeous body sprawled across the duvet. He ran his finger around her nipple as her chest rose and fell. "Stay with me tonight."

Her eyes surveyed his face before she nodded. "Let me freshen up."

He rolled away and pointed to the bathroom. "I don't have anything to wear. What am I going to do for clothes," she asked over her shoulder.

"Who needs clothes?" He followed her. "But if you insist, I'll find something around here."

"I'm not wearing your ex-girlfriend's clothes," she teased. Her quirky grin made his heart speed up. "Don't give me that look, Simeon. I'm serious. I'd rather sleep naked." She swished mouth wash around her mouth then rinsed.

"That's just what I had in mind." He traced a line between her breasts and stopped at her navel. It was well after midnight, but desire had him wide awake.

She shook her head, curls surrounded her face. "I just don't know what's happening with us."

"What do you want to happen?"

She didn't look away. "You know, we're having this serious conversation and I'm naked, I feel disadvantaged."

He didn't hide his erection. "You're blushing."

"You're forward."

"Always, when I see something I want." Hiding his feelings for her was useless now. "I've wanted you for so long. Since that basketball game when you ran onto the court, waving your pom-poms, and hugged me." The wine loosened his tongue, his inhibitions melted away.

He wished he could control his desire, but it was too late. Tonight wasn't about her house, his company, the strip mall, or which side of the tracks they grew up on. Tonight was about them. Over the years, every woman, every acquaintance, every date had been compared to Asa, and so far, no one measured up. No one could. Now that she stood completely nude in his bathroom. Nothing else mattered.

He held out his hand and pulled her closer. Her willingness only accelerated his need. He wrapped his arms around her, held her tight, and buried his nose in her hair. It smelled like flowers. She ran her hand along his back. The slow circles stroked new life into his tense muscles. He layered kisses on her shoulders, her stomach and her thighs as he descended her body. Every nerve in his body screamed to be inside her, to feel the warmth of her body, again. But he slowed his pursuit. He lifted her onto the edge of the bathroom vanity.

"Are you sure this is what you want?" he asked.

She responded by inserting her tongue into his mouth

and making small circles. He continued to tantalize her nub. With each swipe of his finger she increased the pressure on his tongue. Everything he thought he wanted seemed miniscule in comparison to his desire for her. One touch from Asa and he was ready to walk away from everything just to have her. He released her tongue and peered into her eyes. Her eyes were closed, pleasure showed in the planes of her face.

He kissed the soft skin of her neck. She smelled as good as she tasted. He trailed kisses on her shoulder to her breasts. Her nipples hardened against his tongue as his finger slid in and out of her warm folds. With each stroke her moans grew louder and more urgent as he removed his finger, she arched her back and a low continuous moan escaped from her throat. She ran her tongue across his chest. His body trembled as she fastened her fingers around his erection, tugging with enough pressure to send fire racing through his loins.

He backed away, receiving a tiny groan of frustration from Asa, then opened a drawer on the vanity to remove several condoms. He opened one and rolled it into place.

He couldn't wait another moment. Desire tore through him like an express train. He grabbed her hips, pulled her toward the edge of the counter and entered her. Her warm, moist core grabbed him, sucking him deeper. She threw her head back and whispered his name. The intoxicating sound of her voice rang in his ears. He wanted the moment to last, but his need for her shattered his composure. Her nails dug into his back as she repeated his name. The steady crescendo of her voice ended abruptly when she clutched him and pushed her hips forward. The force of her muscles contracting pushed him into oblivion.

His explosive release enveloped him. With his head buried in her neck he surrendered to his love for her.

Tripped up again by Asa. Damn.

Chapter Fifteen

Asa recognized the sensation in her gut as she clung to Simeon. She was falling for him. Again. She refused to soften her grip on him until her body resumed a normal rhythm. She quivered when he buried his head against her neck and kissed her. This was real, not the dream she relived in her head whenever she was lonely.

His kiss warmed the insulation around her heart, melting her protective shield. This was exactly what she wanted. But she didn't need to be in love with someone committed to being single. Her heart thundered in her ears. This same sentiment trapped her in a failed marriage and estranged her from her parents. She tried to swallow the guilt. *Get it together or get in trouble.*

She watched him dispose of the used condoms with one swift move.

Another evening with Simeon couldn't hurt. Just one more. Tomorrow she'd focus.

She wrapped her legs around his waist. His touch started slow, gradually increasing in intensity. She kneaded his back, holding on to him as if he were a lifeline. After invading her thoughts for so long it seemed impossible that he had just screwed her in the family room, solarium and bathroom counter. She wanted to think it was about love, but this had nothing to do with love. She wouldn't get the two confused again.

His tongue flicked her neck, waking her from a two-year slumber. Senses that had been asleep for so long she forgot they existed fired back to life.

Her eyes slid along his muscular body. When they reached his face she held his gaze searching for the meaning in the moment. Were they in a relationship now? Or was tonight just a distraction for him? His eyes revealed nothing.

"I know I promised to be a gentleman tonight, but I couldn't..."

"I'm not complaining," she said. He kissed her gently. His tongue slowly sought hers, encircling her tongue so leisurely it seemed like a taunting dance. She wrapped her arms around his neck.

He grabbed the extra condoms, and then lifted her off the counter. With his hands cradled under her buttocks he carried her into the bedroom. His strides were even and sure. He lowered her onto the bed. She caught her breath. There were more reasons to stop him than there were to surrender to him but she couldn't think of one. His hands massaged her breasts; the warmth of his palm ignited her body. The involuntary arch of her back brought her closer to him. When she tried to pull him on top of her, he pulled back and kissed her shoulders then drew on one nipple, taking his time before moving to the second with the same luxurious motion.

Her hips ground against the soft sheets, a continuous groan rolled from the back of her throat. His actions were slow, not hurried like before. His warm, sensual touch devoured every inch of her. All the dreams or illusions she'd had about him couldn't compare to the fire he sent roaring through her body. She moaned his name.

He continued kissing her body. Between her thighs his

tongue darted into her center with such intensity she bolted upright in the bed, tightening her hold on his ears. His hot tongue stroked her. She grabbed the sheets, balling the Egyptian cotton into her fist.

"Oh, Simeon," she whispered.

He stopped long enough to look in her eyes. The fiery passion in his dark brown eyes didn't match his earlier commitment to remain uninvolved. He murmured something she couldn't hear.

"What?"

Instead of answering he held her gaze. His dark eyes filled with something. Was it lust?

She fell against the pillows. She wanted to read something into the way his palms caressed her stomach or the way his fingertips traced the outline of her breast with a slow, easy touch. But she knew better. Anything he said would be driven by lust, nothing more.

He reached for the foil condoms beside her on the bed. She removed the packet from his hand then, massaged the latex sheath into place. The warmth of his penis set her ablaze.

Then he rose up and straddled her. He slipped into her while his eyes continued to pierce through her. Together they were so natural, it felt like they had been making love for years. He slipped in and out of her, each thrust slower and deeper. She tried to speed up his movement but his powerful hips remained in control. His slow movement strummed her nub. She felt him expand and a wave of ecstasy washed over her like molten lava. Her body tightened around him. Her climax started at her core and rolled across her flesh. Her body contorted with a velocity that lifted her back off the bed, quaking with electrical pulses, before releasing her.

He drove deep into her and his body stiffened. He held her so tight she couldn't move.

"Wow," she whispered.

"Wow is right, but is that it? That's all you're going to say?" He pulled her close and nuzzled his chin into her neck.

"Give me a minute."

They lapsed into a comfortable silence. Music still played downstairs. She should have known the words to the song, but her mind was racing. The lyrics eluded her. How in the world could she ever let him go?

"How much of this did you have planned?"

"Would you believe me if I said none of it?"

"So, you had nothing to do with the mishap with my car?" she teased.

"Nothing at all. That was just my good luck. I couldn't have planned a more perfect evening."

She faced him, propped up on one elbow. Illumination from the bathroom light cast a shadow across his face. "You keep condoms in all your drawers?"

"Well, doesn't every man? Just in case?"

"Uh, huh. Did you think I would be that easy?"

He produced his wicked smile. "I've been waiting for

you for ten years. You're the most evasive woman I know. You take playing hard-to-get to a professional level."

She dropped her head on his chest. "I wasn't playing."

"I didn't think so." He captured her mouth. His tongue was gentle until he deepened the passionate kiss.

With his finger he lifted her chin, drawing her closer. The only thing real was this moment. To think beyond it would erode its beauty. His penis throbbed against her thigh.

"Again?"

"Again, please." The lusty quality in his voice erased everything else from her mind. She closed her eyes and accepted him.

Sometime during the night she heard him get out of bed, turn off the bathroom light and draw the sheet over her. He climbed back in the bed and pulled her close. She settled against his warm body. Sleep slowly descended on her while she listened to him breathe.

§ § §

The room was drenched in sunlight when Simeon lifted his head off the pillow and rubbed his temples. It wasn't a dream. Finally, he had his princess. If only he could set the time back a few hours and enjoy it all again. His cock hardened as he gazed at her ethereal beauty and silky skin. Without waking Asa he swung his legs off the bed and rested his chin in the palms of his hand. The pounding in his head was so loud he couldn't hear his own thoughts. He staggered out of the bedroom.

How long could Asa throw him off his game? Trying to manage his emotions for her was about as stupid as pretending to ignore her throughout high school. He could negotiate with powerful, demanding people easier than he could face how he felt about her.

In the bathroom he found aspirin in his medicine cabinet. He took two with a long gulp of water before staring at his reflection in the mirror. Get it together, man. You know kryptonite when you see it.

After a full minute, he pushed off the Italian marble countertop and headed back to the bedroom. Asa was sound asleep, breathing so softly only the rise and fall of her exposed breast showed any sign of life. She was an angel.

He ran his hands across the top of his head. Now what? What was supposed to happen now? He dressed in a pair of khaki shorts and an army green t-shirt before heading to his office. It took a few moments to locate the number of his personal mechanic. He made arrangements for him to fix her car.

Coffee. He needed coffee to clear his head. A stiff cup of java would help him think straight. He filled the teapot for Asa.

He hoped she didn't think last night changed things between them. As much as he wanted to settle down and do the whole family thing, it was too lame for him. He had no intentions of misleading her. He pulled bacon and eggs from the refrigerator.

The whole night was his idea. As always he controlled his actions.

"What smells so good?" Asa stood in the doorway. Her face was scrubbed clean and her unruly hair had been pulled back into a thick ponytail. She wore his oversized blue and gold shirt that barely covered her shapely ass.

"Good morning, sleepyhead. He raked scrambled eggs onto a platter. "I hope you're hungry, I've cooked enough to feed a small army."

"I should get going."

"You don't have a car." He nodded at her to take a seat at the table.

"I can call Dakota to pick me up and have the car towed later."

He sat across from her at the kitchen table. Even without make-up Asa was stunning. Instead of looking sleep deprived, she glowed. There was a softness to her that made him want to sweep her into his arms and take her back upstairs. He wished he could give her what she wanted, but his promise to his mother came first.

"Asa, I'll have Dewy look at your car. And I'll take you home after you eat."

"Who's Dewy?"

"My mechanic. I called him first thing this morning."

"You have your own mechanic? A mechanic that makes house calls? How do you even know where my car is right now?"

"Believe me, it is probably still sitting in front of the mission. This isn't as fancy as dinner, but it's tolerable." He pointed to the plate in front of her.

She lifted the eggs to her mouth but put the fork down without tasting them. "You're actually a very good cook, but these eggs are runny." She used her fork to point at the plate. "Simeon, I can't let you pay to have my car fixed. I can handle it. I can take care of myself."

"Whoa, Asa. I don't doubt you can take care of yourself. I was only trying to be helpful. If it's about the money..."

"It's not the money. These are the kinds of things I need to step up and work out. I don't want to be dependent on anyone else. I just went through that and..." She jumped up.

"Let Dewy fix your car. I'll give you a lift home and if it makes you feel any better you can pay me back."

When she started to object, he raised his hands. "It's the least I can do. It's the most efficient way to get this resolved. Besides you're hardly dressed to take care of any business this morning."

He read the reluctance in her eyes, her petite frame oozed defiance.

"I can get dressed in minutes. That's not the issue." She crossed her arms and the shirt rose slightly almost exposing the intersection of her thighs.

"Are you going to finish your breakfast?"

She flopped in the chair next to him and moved the food around on her plate without eating.

"I was trying to be helpful," he offered.

I know." She looked up at him. "And thank you for

your help b-but...I promised myself when I moved back here that I wouldn't depend on anyone. Not even my sisters. Especially not my sisters."

"Trust me. I know how hard it is to change perceptions." The doorbell rang. "I wonder who that is." He stood, crossed the room and spoke into the intercom. "Yeah?"

"I have a package from the Plaid Group for Simeon Harper of Harper Enterprise."

Simeon stole a quick glance at her. He ran his hand over his head. "I'll be right there. Just a minute."

With Asa's eyes riveted on him, he hurried from the room.

Another hole I'll need to get out of.

Chapter Sixteen

"I thought you said no business." She called to Simeon before he headed for the door.

"I'll be right back."

She pushed the runny eggs to the side of the plate and nibbled a piece of bacon. The crispy meat crumbled in her mouth. The bacon was perfectly cooked.

She envied Simeon's ability to focus on one thing with such intensity. His world revolved around his work and everything else seemed secondary. Some part of him was off limits to her. That much was very clear. Getting involved with Simeon meant being in second place. Again.

She scraped the remnants of the food into the trash before clearing the rest of the table. Simeon's hushed conversation floated in from the foyer. She could hear a few words; contract, funds, signature.

Guilt washed over her. Eavesdropping was akin to stealing in her grandmother's eyes. So she turned on the water to rinse the dishes then loaded the dishwasher. The noise drowned out Simeon's discussion.

She examined the tidy kitchen before heading up the back stairs. She needed a shower and clothes.

In the bedroom, she discarded his shirt and stepped into the marble shower. Warm water pelted her shoulders and splattered her face. She sighed, allowing the water to wash away the remnants of last night. Maybe she was hypersensitive. Snapping at Simeon for trying to help with her car wasn't called for. She buried her head under the water spray and rolled her shoulders.

"Ah, there you are." Simeon stood outside the glass enclosure, pulling off his clothes. "I hope you don't mind if I join you."

He stepped in before she could answer and dropped a condom on the shower seat. He turned on the opposite showerhead before spinning to face her. Water bounced off his chest while a stream trailed down his abs and disappeared in his pubic hair. His strong jaw displayed a hint of stubble making him look rugged. She would never grow tired of looking at him.

His hands explored her soapy breasts. "Simeon..."

"Shh...I can't get enough of you." He found her mouth. His warm tongue darted inside, quieting her comment.

Her tongue met his enthusiasm. Her body wanted him even as her head cautioned her to slow down. He massaged the soap against her skin then cupped his hands, filling them with water to rinse the soap off. When his mouth found her nipples they hardened under his touch. She wobbled, his thick arms held on to her, cradling her against the smooth marble.

She reached for his erection as it pulsed against her flesh, hot and hard. She tightened her hand around his penis.

He moaned with pleasure, and then released her nipple. "Do you want me?" he whispered in her ear.

Words wouldn't come. She nodded.

"Say it. Say you want me." His eyes blazed with a heat that matched hers.

She swallowed. "Yes. Yes, Simeon, I want you." Her voice sounded thick.

He dropped to his knees and inserted his tongue inside her. She shuddered. His tongue burrowed deeper, drawing in and out agonizingly slow and steady. Her heart responded, swelling to accept her love for him. He devoured her like prey, each thrust willing her to surrender. She closed her eyes; his tongue drove her insane. Steam from the shower rose around them, adding to their heat. Her orgasm started with a flicker before ripping through her body and exploding into tiny pieces. He held her while she shook with pleasure. Then he placed his tongue in her mouth. She tasted the residue of her essence. He released a primal growl that vibrated in her ears.

Without releasing her tongue, he lifted her against the marbled wall and slipped his sheathed penis inside her. He pushed his tongue deeper into her mouth. The only sound in the room was the rhythmic patter of the water hitting the river rock on the shower floor.

§ § §

"I can't believe I'm dressed before you," she teased from the chaise while she watched him.

"You didn't have anything to choose from. You were going to wear your clothes from yesterday or go home naked. And you wouldn't have gotten very far if you attempted the latter."

She grinned at him. "So, what was that all about this

morning?"

He walked into the dressing room without looking at her. "What?"

"With the courier and all, I thought you said no business. I kept my promise about no business...but you..."

"That vow was for last night. Besides that only applied to you, not to me and Harper Enterprise. I can't always stop the business clock."

Asa swung her feet off the chaise and stalked to the entrance of his dressing room. His back was to the door. The muscles in his shoulders bulged. "So your business always comes first?"

"Always." He pulled on a shirt before facing her.

"And what about us?"

"Oh, I enjoy you." He grinned. "I'll always make time for you."

"Uh-huh. As long as I don't interfere with business, right?"

He grabbed her hips and pulled her close. "You won't, just like I wouldn't interfere with your work." He kissed her cheek and led her out of the bedroom.

She didn't need to see his eyes to know he was keeping something from her. Being married to Eric had taught her well. She understood living on the fringe of someone's life.

§ § §

Simeon caught a glimpse of Asa from the corner of his eye as he drove toward the city. She chewed her thumbnail, her body purposely turned away from him.

"Okay, don't tell me you're still upset because I stepped in to get your car fixed or because I conducted a little business this morning."

"I'm not upset.'

"I didn't mean to throw off your plan to do everything yourself," Simeon said.

"You're pretty good at doing that."

"You weren't complaining last night...or this morning." He leveled his gaze at her.

"No, not at all and I'm not complaining now. Last night was... last night--"

"Why are you so quiet?"

"I'm just processing some of the things we talked about. How about we say it was a nice evening," she said.

"Nice? I put some of my best moves on you and you give me nice?"

"You have some pretty smooth moves." She nodded. "But I'm not twenty. I'm looking for more than good sex."

"I told you I'm not looking."

"So, we're at odds again. That's the norm for us, isn't it?"

They continued the ride without talking. How could he tell her about the project? The subject of his project was off limits last night, but to continue the charade any further was deceitful. She must have overheard the exchange with the courier.

Her house sat at the end of his wrecking ball. He doubted she understood the importance of his project. He was a success. Something his father was never able to do.

He pulled the car into an empty space in front of her house. "Asa, if I can do anything for you..." He turned off the ignition.

She turned in her seat and focused her attention on him. "If you want to do something for me, don't tear down my house."

His stomach constricted. There was no way to sidestep her this time. He held her gaze for several moments before speaking. "That's not an option, Asa." This was the conversation he'd dreaded. The destruction of her home was inevitable. Nothing, not even Asa, would change his mind about the project.

"Then tell me what you're hiding from me." She straightened in her seat.

He continued to look into her eyes.

"Why are you pretending you want to do something for me? I only wanted one thing from you. I need my house."

Simeon gripped the steering wheel with both hands. "Look Asa, don't twist this into something it's not. We had a really good time last night, but please don't think that means I want your advice on how to run my business."

"I'm not trying to run your business. I'm asking you to help me." She turned toward the house. "Now that you're wealthy, I'm sure you can have anything you want. You have plenty of money, a big house—you even have your own personal mechanic. The only thing I have is this house. Even though it means nothing to you, it means the world to me." Asa sat back, her shoulders stiff with anger.

"Just because you've shown up after several years, you expect me to change my plans?"

Her eyes narrowed, gleaming with unshed tears. Her bottom lip trembled. Simeon prepared for the barrage that was coming.

"The courier this morning, was that about your strip mall?" She glared at him.

"As a matter of fact it was. I signed the contract to release the funds this morning."

She tilted her chin up. "Then what did you do, Simeon—run upstairs to make love...to have sex with me? Did that make you feel better? Was it supposed to make me feel better?" Her voice was barely audible. "You know, Simeon..." She pulled her hair back. "I thought you'd changed. But you're still that mean, angry boy from high school. Back then I was scared of you, scared to approach you. I'm not that little girl anymore." She grabbed the door handle.

"Asa, wait."

"Why?"

"Let's talk."

"We're beyond talk." She turned toward him. "How much time do I have?"

"A few weeks...maybe a month." She stepped out of the car, slamming the door so hard it jolted him.

Her shoulders squared as she walked up the stairs. He grabbed the driver's side door handle. The steel cooled his hand. There wasn't anything he could say that would change where they were.

§ § §

Asa closed the door to the house with the same force she used on his car.

What had she expected? For him to save her house because she loved him? Because she slept with him...because she asked him? When she left Atlanta she was supposed to leave stupidity behind, but some habits were hard to break.

She fought back the sob that rose in her throat. Crying wouldn't change anything. It was time to put her plan to work. Nobody could save her. She had to save herself.

Scruffy ran out of the kitchen at full speed. His high-pitched yelp made her smile as he skidded into her.

"Asa, is that you?" Dakota came around the corner.

She stopped petting the dog and sighed. She didn't want to see her sister right now. She swiped her eyes with the back of her hands. "I didn't expect to see you this morning."

"So, you spent the night with Simeon, huh?" Dakota placed her hands on her hips and looked down at her sister.

"I had car trouble and couldn't get home."

"That's a convenient excuse, but not one you should be proud of."

"Please, Dakota, not now. The last thing I need is a lecture. "

"Fine, Asa, but remember this is a small town. People in this neighborhood don't have much going on, so they like to talk. Simeon is not some unknown man, everybody in the city knows him."

"I don't want to talk about Simeon." Asa turned away from her sister.

"You've been crying. What happened?" Dakota reached for her.

"I'm fine. Really, I'm fine."

"Then why are your eyes red?"

"Dakota, leave it alone. I'm fine."

Asa dropped her purse on the couch. "Where do we stand on the rally?" Asa asked. "And if you have something negative to say about the rally, don't. Just don't."

Dakota raised one brow. "I think everything is in place. I made some calls last night. A few shop owners have agreed to donate food. The banner will be ready in a few days. You just need to make sure your friend Lara will be there. I've told everyone about the TV cameras. Don't make a liar out of me."

"They'll be there." Asa nodded.

"Did you tell Simeon about your plan?"

"I don't owe Simeon anything. And I'd rather he not

know about it."

"He might get wind of what's going on. Then what?"

"By then everything will be planned and he can't stop us. I'm leaving for New York on Monday to meet with suppliers and show organizers. I'll be gone for several days, we'll have the rally next Saturday. It doesn't have to be big or extravagant."

"I've gotten several calls from folks in the neighborhood. They like the idea. They hope you can make a difference, but are you sure you want to do this." Dakota searched her eyes.

"I have to. It's my last stand."

"You know Custer didn't survive his last stand?"

And I might not survive Simeon.

Chapter Seventeen

The whirlwind of the New York trip had done little to ease the stabbing ache in her heart. "Serves you right for being so gullible."

Asa sat at her kitchen table to scanned the list, checking off items with her red pen. Everything was in place. Simeon couldn't do anything to stop the rally now. With any luck, he didn't even know what she had planned. She folded the piece of paper and slipped it into the pocket of her shorts.

Her plan to get the community involved in stopping his project might not save her house, but at least she hadn't curled up in bed and cried. Fighting for something felt so much better than giving in. Putting her life back together was worth every nail clawing, back breaking effort she could think of.

The last time she saw Simeon the dark, fiery look in his eyes made her wonder how far he would go for his project. At least he never misled her. Never once did he let her think her house was safe. She smiled as she admired his honesty. But she knew he wouldn't change his mind.

From the window she watched while Scruffy sniffed the hydrangea in the back yard and then she scrolled through her cell phone log. No calls from Simeon since he dropped her off a week ago. She wanted to call him, to hear his voice, or feel his arms around her, but that was silly. His position was clear, it always had been.

She ran her thumb over the screen. The log was full. Eric's name appeared twice. She studied the phone for several moments then shrugged her shoulders. Life was cruel.

Her cell phone vibrated. Eric's number blared at her. She didn't answer. When the phone quieted she deleted his number from the phone then blocked his calls.

She closed the phone just as it vibrated again.

"Are we all ready for the big rally?" asked Dakota.

She sighed. "It starts in an hour. And thanks to all your hard work we're ready." Asa spotted the dog as he raised his leg against the sad looking bush. She snapped her fingers to get Scruffy's attention. "Thanks for all your support. I know you think I'm nuts, but--"

"I want to support you and based on the number of calls I'm getting you have a lot of people that agree with you. So if you want the house, I don't want Simeon to tear it down, either."

"I'm in a good place. No matter what happens I feel good because at least I'm doing something to help myself. Here in Bristol I don't feel like I have to prove myself.

"You never had to prove yourself to those that love you, Asa," Dakota offered. "Did you call the councilman?"

"The earliest I could get an appointment is next week," Asa said. "A lot of good that will do me."

"What time do you want me at the rally?"

"I'm heading down there in a few minutes. Come early, I can always use help setting up."

"Okay, I should be there in about thirty minutes."

Asa ended the call and gathered everything she needed.

She held the car door open for the dog. He hopped into the passenger seat. Her car had been in front of her house when she returned from New York.

No note.

No call.

No card.

Simeon probably had someone drop it off. She should have called to thank him, but she refused to dial his number. Instead, she sent him a check for the new radiator. This way she owed him nothing.

A tingle of guilt ran along her spine for inviting Simeon's brother, Brian, to the rally. But he insisted on helping when she called to thank him for his help with the car. Brian was easy to talk to and valued community.

She pulled her car into the parking lot. The park was crowded already. This was a good sign. A huge turnout was bound to get attention. It would look great for the media coverage.

Scruffy yanked at his leash as Asa walked to the entrance of the park. She heard her neighbor, Mrs. Donald's hearty laugh drifting across the field, but she couldn't see the stout woman. A flash of warm air blew over her as happy memories of the block parties awakened in her. The smell of food, the laughter, the festive chatter all rushed back as if the last block party had taken place only few days ago. She half expected to see her grandfather and father standing behind a charcoal grill turning hot dogs and hamburgers.

The vision vanished just as quickly as it had come

when she spotted Mrs. Donald instructing the caterer how to set up the food table. The caterer's lip disappeared behind a frown.

Before Asa could rescue the woman Brian Harper stopped her. "There you are."

"Brian, I'm so glad you could make it."

"It was nice of you to allow the men at the mission to come along. They don't often get invited to private affairs."

"You all helped me with the car, I wanted to say thank you again." Asa leaned closer to him and asked, "Did you..."

"No, I didn't mention anything to Simeon. I'll let you and him work that out."

She sighed with relief. "Thank you for keeping my secret. I don't think he would have liked this idea."

"I'm sure of that."

"It won't cause any problems between you, will it?"

"I'm the older brother. It's nothing I can't handle. But if you really want to thank me and the mission, we're always looking for volunteers. If you can fit a few hours into your busy schedule we'd really appreciate a helping hand."

"Between the rally and the organizers of Fashion Week, I've been busy, but I'll be there next week. I'll even try to drag my sister along with me.

Before he could reply they were interrupted. Two rally supporters rolled out the banner. Golden Leaf Community danced across the white batting in thick green letters. "Where do you want us to hang the banner?"

Asa pointed to a cluster of trees at the entrance of the park. "Hang it there. String it from one tree to the next, so everyone can see it as they walk up."

As she talked to the supporters, Brian walked away. His shoulders were as broad as his brother's, but his demeanor was a little more relaxed than Simeon's. He smiled more easily. There was a contentment in his eyes that she never saw with Simeon.

"Asa, can you come over here and tell us where you want these pies?" Mrs. Donald called to her from a group of women gathered around the table. Mrs. Donald reminded her of Mim. The party couldn't start until the food table was just right.

Asa hurried to settle the pie argument. "The caterer can handle all of this. I'm sure whatever she decides will be fine." She rubbed her hand along Mrs. Donald's back hoping to relax the older woman.

"Your caterer is fine, but Meryl from the church brought this pie anyway. Honey, look at this here apple pie. Meryl brought this pie and sat it in the middle of the table like it was some kind of prize. What little crust it has is burned. It looks about as runny as soup. We can't serve this."

"Well..." Asa wasn't certain how to respond. She didn't know Meryl. She didn't want to hurt the feeling of anyone that was nice enough to help make the rally successful. "Well, let's cut it. We can scrape off the burned part. I'm sure it'll be okay."

Mrs. Donald gave her a skeptical look. "You just don't want to hurt her feelings do you?"

"I really don't."

"Okay, we'll do things your way, but if anyone asks me for pie, I'm going to tell them to eat the peach or blueberry cobbler instead." Mrs. Donald stuck her knife in the pie like she was butchering a piece of meat.

"Look, the camera crew has arrived." Asa motioned to the front gate. "Can you handle this?"

"Yeah, baby, I got this." She waved Asa away. "You go ahead."

Asa scurried to the other side of the park.

"Oh good, Asa, there you are," the news anchor said. "We're going to set up right here. We'll want to talk with a few of the neighbors first and we'll talk with you last." She waved a clipboard at her crew. "I also want to get a few shots of the area. It looks great. We'll be live for the early news and then run a clip of the event on the evening segment."

"Thank you for doing this."

"It's not a problem. We needed a human interest piece tonight. We're always looking for local stuff that our viewers might be interested in. Once I heard your story, I thought the rally might make a good segment." She looked around. "You've done your part of getting the people here. It's a nice crowd."

"I think this crowd will send a message."

"Have you had any luck talking the developer into

changing his plans?"

Asa bit down on her lip. After several dates with Simeon, she was no closer to understanding him or negotiating with him. "No, no change. So I'm counting on you to make this good."

"I'll do my best, sweetie. Go greet your guests and I'll come find you shortly."

§ § §

Simeon dropped his pen and sat back in the chair. The house was too quiet. Deathly quiet. He massaged his temples. A tension headache was mounting an attack behind his eyes.

He opened the folder on the desk. Everything was in order, his neat, tidy project. He pulled open the top drawer to his file cabinet, plucked through the files until he found the one labeled location alternatives. His finger rolled down the list of parcels of land that had been under consideration for the strip mall. One particular lot was larger, but more expensive and further away. He hunched over the specifications for a closer look.

His pulse raced. He sat back in the chair. His skin prickled with interest. After a slow, measured breath he snatched open his desk drawer and took out his protractor and surveys. With the point pressed firmly in the drawing he measured the distance from both parcels of land. Switching the strip mall to the new site produced possibilities. It provided access to more people. Selecting the Golden Leaf Community had been easy, maybe too easy. A bitter taste formed in his mouth. He'd never intended to bully his way into Golden Leaf. Business was never personal, but maybe this time, this project came too close.

Maybe she was right. There was an alternative worth considering. He picked up the phone to call her, but placed the receiver back in the cradle. They hadn't spoken in over a week. He hadn't even bothered to call her about the car. She wanted more than he could give. Moving the project to a new location didn't mean they would settle in for happily-ever-after. But at least he could offer her some hope about her house.

This news he had to deliver in person. He raced to the kitchen, grabbed his keys and jumped in the car. He chose the sporty Porsche. This wasn't a leisurely drive. The sooner he shared his news with Asa, the sooner he could stop feeling like the Grinch that stole her Christmas joy. He shifted into fourth gear as he neared the turnpike. The thought of seeing her radiant smile and hearing her soft voice were enough to turn him on.

His phone rang. He hit the voice control command, "Yeah, Simeon here."

"This is George, from The Plaid Group."

"Hello, George, what can I do for you?" Simeon turned onto Route 100 without tapping his brake. "Did you receive the contract?"

"Do you know about this rally?"

"What are you talking about?" The tone of George's voice made his chest tighten. He pulled onto the shoulder of the road. "I don't like guessing games, what are you talking about?"

"There's a rally taking place right now in the park near Golden Leaf. I don't think it's in support of the project. We don't need negative publicity just as we're getting ready to break ground. It makes the backers nervous."

Simeon closed his eyes. His free hand massaged his brow. "There's nothing to worry about, George."

"You're sure?"

"George, this is not the first time you've done business with Harper Enterprise. You know how I operate. You have nothing to worry about."

"That's what I figured."

"We'll talk Monday." Simeon ended the call. He sat frozen for several moments as cars sped past. He snorted. His fingers clenched the steering wheel baring his knuckles. This stunt had Asa Conroy written all over it.

After several deep breaths, he punched the accelerator and headed for Golden Leaf. He knew exactly what was going on and who was behind it.

Simeon rounded the corner of Buchanan Street. His car rims scraped the curb before screeching to a halt. He drummed his palm on the steering wheel as he tried to stem the anger igniting in his stomach. He searched the enormous crowd for Asa. The Conroy stamp was on this event from the banner, the music and the food. This might as well be one of their damned block parties.

He continued to drum the steering wheel, each slap harder than the last. He swallowed the bile rising from his stomach. Had Asa intentionally betrayed him? Did she think he would give in to her because of this rally? Sitting in the car, watching from a distance was like observing ghosts from his past. The battle in his heart churned up feelings of emptiness, of not being good enough, that should have been gone.

Up ahead, he spotted Asa walking to the park entrance with that reporter from the local network. He watched her gesture to the crowd and point to the huge banner draped across the entrance to the park. Asa laughed at something, her face lit up with a radiant smile. It was time to confront this situation, head on.

After a final smack of the steering wheel, he barreled out of the car. Without taking his eyes off Asa he crossed the court. There was no way to know how this would end, but her betrayal carved a hole in his heart. Anger and disappointment guided his steps. Forget the new parcel of land. Everything would go back to the original plan. Nothing could stand in his way of taking down that block now. The city needed the planned community and senior center and he intended to make sure he gave them what they needed.

"Asa, I need to talk to you," Simeon's voice boomed across the park. She jumped. Activity stopped.

She frowned but signaled for him to wait while she continued to talk with the reporter. He shifted his weight and scratched his forehead. His heart roared in his chest, threatening to force its way out. Several deep breaths did nothing to calm him. He shoved his hands in his pockets and stared at Asa.

She ignored his gesture and took her time.

Simeon folded his arms across his chest. One long breath. Another long one and he felt his Hulk-like demeanor diminish. There was no sense making a scene, so he allowed her a moment. Waiting was one of his virtues; most of his adult life had been spent waiting. He walked away from the crowd.

After the camera crew packed up their equipment and drove off in the news van, Asa stomped toward him.

"Can you tell me why you're yelling at me?" She stood in front of him with her hands planted on her hips. Her eyes blazed like hot coals.

"What is this?" He swung his arms wide to encompass the park. "Is this supposed to make me change my mind? Do you think a block party will make me change my mind? You've been gone years, now all of a sudden you're back and everybody is supposed to redirect their life because you said so?" His didn't try to stop the rage from entering his voice.

"Why do you think all these people are here? They're here because they care about this community. They care about their homes. If you weren't so arrogant you'd see that."

"What I see is deception. Were you planning this all along?"

"No, but you left me no choice. I had to do something."

"What do you expect to accomplish? Am I supposed to change my mind now?"

She scowled at him but didn't respond.

"I stayed behind, Asa. Everything I've done has been for the benefit of this community. The strip mall will give the people a place to shop without having to drive or catch a bus to the other side of town. Do you have any idea where the closest grocery store is?"

Asa averted her eyes, then he continued. "Do you know that some of these people, your neighbors, go weeks without fresh fruit or vegetables because they have no transportation across town? So don't think you're so high and mighty because you pulled together a little block party." He lowered his voice, but the rage remained.

"It's not a party, it's a rally. A rally to let you and everyone know we love this neighborhood and we don't want you to tear it down." There was an edge in her voice. "We don't want to be pushed out of our homes."

The slow hum of a chant rose from the crowd. "Save Golden Leaf. Save Golden Leaf." The chant crescendoed, rolling across the park like thunder. Some participants threw their fists into the air. He shoved his hands in his pocket until the rebellion slowed to a soft rumble by a few diehards. A group of older women glared motherly disapproval at him. The same kind he'd seen in his mother's eyes when he was being difficult.

Simeon grabbed her hand to turn their backs to the crowd. "Th—this—" he snapped his fingers. "We can make this work out." He lowered his voice.

The determined look in her eyes smoldered with defiance. Beneath her stare was a hint of pain, her sparkle was gone. Her bottom lip trembled for a second before she grabbed it with her teeth. An urge to pull her into his arms rushed over him. There had to be a way to make this work for everybody. Her fiery temper gave him no room to think.

"Look, Asa, I'm not trying to hurt you." He rubbed the goosebumps on her arms, his tone softer now.

"Well, what are you trying to do? You charged into the park like a snorting bull. You must have wanted to accomplish something. Were you trying to intimidate me? Do you want me to go running back to Atlanta? Or would you prefer I get out of your life in general?"

Her brown eyes pierced his. The chanting stopped. He turned around to survey the thick crowd. A few people continued to stare at them. He wanted to share his news with her, but this wasn't the setting. "Can we talk later? I'll come by your house."

Simeon looked up to see his brother striding toward him.

"Simeon, are you okay?"

"Brian-- What...what are you doing here?"

"Asa invited me and the guys from the mission."

Simeon looked from his brother back to Asa. His stomach dropped. Brian held up his hands. "Whoa, Simeon, it's not like that."

He faced his brother. "Explain it to me then."

"I asked him not to tell you." Asa stepped closer to Simeon. "I didn't want you to interfere with the plans."

"I see.

"I just go where I'm needed and help where I can. You

know that, brother."

"What I know is my brother betrayed me." He turned to Asa. "And you asked him to."

That woman is so infuriating and I let her under my skin.

Chapter Eighteen

Dakota turned off the car. "Are you sure you want to do this?" She nodded to the front door of the mission where a man and woman reclined against the stucco building smoking a cigarette.

"I promised Brian I'd do this, and I will." Asa shifted toward her sister. "Thank you for agreeing to come with me. I get the impression they can always use an extra pair of hands."

Dakota turned her gaze back to the mission door. "Have you heard from Simeon yet? He looked pretty angry when he stalked away from the rally last week."

"No. I'm sure he thinks I'm the devil reincarnated. He thinks I turned his brother against him."

Dakota squeezed her hand and held on, not letting go. "What's next after this?" She nodded to the mission door again. "Does it mean you're giving up...on saving the house, I mean?"

"I remember when you used to be the savior of lost causes. I always wondered why you didn't give up. Now, I understand. I never cared about anything so much until now. This is home. It's the place where Mom and I weren't at odds with each other. Until moving back I felt like a failure."

"It takes two to make a marriage work," said Dakota.

"I'm not just talking about my marriage. Maybe it wasn't a good idea to come back here and get involved with Simeon either. What was I thinking?"

"Stop beating yourself up. Curiosity gets the best of all of us, sometimes. And as good looking as he is, I can see why you crumbled."

"But you'll be pleased to know, I asked my realtor to find me a condo near the studio." Asa looked off, into the distance. "He called last night and he has something for me to look at."

"Give it a little time. You'll be okay. When your designs make it to Bryant Park, you won't have time for that big old house anyway. You'll be too busy jet-setting around."

"Yeah, I need to focus on the show and opening the shop."

Asa released her sister's hand. "We better get inside. A line is starting to form."

The activity level in the mission dining room mirrored organized chaos. Asa motioned for her sister to follow as she weaved through the maze of tables.

"Excuse me, we're here to volunteer. Can you tell me who I need to see?" Asa asked a man blocking the aisle.

"See Miss Kitty, she's over there. The one in the apron." He stepped aside and allowed her and Dakota to pass.

Asa made the introductions over the clanking of plates in the kitchen. Miss Kitty stood five feet tall but looked strong enough to manage the huge pots. Her blonde hair hung to her waist but her vivid blue eyes were what caught Asa's attention.

"You two don't look as big as one of our platters, but

we're glad to have you. Follow me and I'll get you set up. She led them down a hall to a side door. "Have either of you ever worked here before?"

"I've helped out before, but it's been a few years," Dakota responded.

"This is my first time," Asa replied.

"It doesn't matter. Here are your aprons. Wash your hands over there. When you're ready, go through that door. It leads back to the staging area. We'll put you right to work. There are a lot of hungry people to feed tonight." Miss Kitty walked out of the room.

In the staging area a man with large hands pointed to a counter containing five cakes.

"Cut these cakes then place them on those plates. You should get ten slices from each one. If you don't you're cutting them too big." He pointed to an empty counter. "There's space for you over there. You two look alike. Are you twins?"

"No, we're not twins." Dakota picked up the knife.

He grunted. "Well, do you think you can handle this?"

Asa moved to the quiet table, relieved her assignment wasn't more complicated. Absent-minded activity suited her fine. A weight settled on her shoulders when she asked the agent to find her a condo. But facing reality had kindled new energy into her. Last night her sketches had been more fluid and carefree. Hopefully, Dakota was right and she would be able to move on.

One day, maybe Simeon would be able to forgive her for the stunt at the park. The irritation in his eyes still haunted her. He had a right to be angry. In the dim light of the mission kitchen guilt rose in her throat and threatened her air flow. But hurting Simeon in the process was never a part of the plan. She sighed as she pressed the knife through the dense cake.

The smell of fried chicken filled the air. Her mouth watered. Maybe her appetite had finally decided to return.

In the corner, a woman wearing a hairnet mixed a large bowl of instant mashed potatoes. Everyone in the kitchen moved with efficiency. They were experienced, not volunteers right off the street like her, but she felt welcome.

Keeping her hands busy left little opportunity to dwell on unhappy thoughts. Work on the design studio ended a week ago. The results were better than expected. The grand opening was scheduled for early September. Several of her customers were flying in for the event. Her designs for Fashion Week were ready for the final model fitting. The silk organza for the finale only needed beading then it would be complete. At least something was going right. Life was almost as good as it was when she was seventeen. Almost.

Exhaustion nipped at her heels. Stopping or slowing down invited hours to think about Simeon, which proved to be futile. Dreaming was a waste. Trying to save the house had soaked up too much precious time already.

"Well, you kept your promise." Brian strolled across the dining room. He kissed her on the cheek. Her heart clenched. His smile reminded her so much of Simeon that she wanted to touch his face.

She averted her eyes. "You didn't doubt me, did you?"

"Well, I did a little. After that blow-up in the park I thought you might want to stay away from the Harper family."

She tried to smile. "I want to be here. Really." She turned to her sister. "Do you know my sister Dakota?"

"You own the book store don't you?"

"Yes." Dakota shook his hand. "Oh, by the way, Simeon is stopping by tonight. He's started speaking to me again."

Asa looked around the crowded dining room, half expecting to see Simeon's cold stare in the crowd. "I'm sorry if I caused you any trouble—"

"It's no big deal. Simeon is just misunderstood. Our childhood was a little disjointed and he's still trying to deal with—" He gestured with his hands. "He's trying to deal with the dysfunction and the imaginary black-eye on the family name."

Asa nodded. "Simeon must think I'm some spoiled little girl. I've taken my childhood for granted. It was so easy, growing up in the shadow of love from both my parents and grandparents." She clasped her hands. "His childhood left him scarred and mine left me naïve." His need to tear down the houses in Golden Leaf must have been festering like a wound for years.

She tried to expel the vision he must have of her. Was there any way they both could be happy? The sweet road home for her had been idyllic. But her return had to be less than ideal for him.

"He won't get here until well after the dinner hour. He comes in after he leaves the office so it will be very late. You should be long gone by then."

"Thanks, Brian. I don't think it's a good idea for me to run into him. It seems like we always find something to bicker about and...and I don't want to spar with him today."

"Fair enough. It was nice to see you again, Dakota." He eyed Dakota quickly before leaving the dining room.

"What was that all about?" Asa asked her sister.

"What?"

"You can't fool me, Dakota."

"I'm not trying to fool you."

"Did I pick up on something going on between you two?"

"No. So leave it alone."

§ § §

Simeon closed the file folder on his desk. His eyes stung. Reading contracts all day was grueling. He'd rather visit a work site than sit behind a desk. But renegotiating contracts required diligence. He stifled a yawn. The traffic lights outside his window caught his eye. It was too cloudy to see the skyline so he leaned against the windowsill and stared down at the snarled traffic below. The light changed several times before he pulled his attention away.

He moved back to his desk and lifted the receiver on the phone. He wanted to talk to Asa. With the phone suspended in mid-air, he hesitated. What could he say? He dropped it back in the cradle. The last time he saw her, she was spitting fire and even that enticed him. He closed his eyes and massaged his temples.

He snatched the phone off the hook when it rang, hoping it was Asa. He sighed seeing Brad's name on the caller ID.

"Simeon, Brad Stevens here. I just wanted you to know that we're set. The cranes and wrecking crews have been rescheduled and we're still on target at the Philadelphia site."

"Good, Brad. Any word yet on the results of that final survey for the strip mall?"

"Not yet. I should know in a few days, but I don't foresee any issues. "

Simeon hung up the phone and glanced out the window. His breathing was uneven. In the last few days all of his time had been spent on saving the Conroy house. He shook his head. Why bother? It wouldn't change anything between them. Life was fine until Asa Conroy moved back to Bristol. He used to control his world. He knew what was going to happen and when.

He grabbed his briefcase and headed out the door. The huge office felt tight and stuffy. He needed fresh air.

"Catherine, I'm leaving for the night."

She glanced at the clock. "Good. Your restlessness is driving me crazy. If you opened that file cabinet one more time I was going to put you in it," she chuckled.

"That bad, huh?"

"Worse. The last few weeks you seemed distracted. I thought you would be happy with the turn of events."

"Umph. If you need me, you know how to reach me."

§ § §

He picked up a bottle of wine before heading to the shelter. Tonight he needed to celebrate the progress of his project with the only person that understood how much it meant to him.

Simeon pulled into the parking lot behind the mission. A line of people waited to get inside. One young boy stood next to his mother, his vacant eyes cast on the pavement. That was him. Those were his eyes, his hunger. Simeon went inside.

"You're as bad as me, working all day," Simeon said as he entered his brother's office.

Brian shot out of his seat and embraced him. Simeon saw his eyes dart toward the dining room. "You're early Sim, I didn't expect you until much later."

"I had to get out of the office." Simeon took the chair in front of the desk. "The walls were closing in on me. I brought a bottle of wine. I was hoping you'd celebrate with me." Simeon pulled the bottle from the bag. "I know this is the last thing the men out there need to see." Simeon nodded to the dining room.

"Sim, you know I don't drink," Brian shook his head.

"I know. But business is good. Philadelphia

construction starts in a few days. I wanted to celebrate with someone who understands my dream.”

“You deserve to toast your success. But Dad did enough drinking to last me a lifetime. I’ve got some soda here.” He pulled a bottle of ginger ale from the refrigerator. “This is bubbly enough for me.”

Simeon nodded. “Dad had a lasting impact on us, huh?”

“I guess so.” Brian popped the lid. “Dad’s the reason I do this work. The reason you do what you do. And the reason our sister hasn’t stepped foot in Bristol since she was eighteen. If I can help one of these men, it makes me feel better. Dad needed a place like this.”

“Do you think he would have gone?”

“No. No way.”

Brian returned to the desk with two glasses. “Sorry I don’t have champagne flutes, but these should work.”

They sipped in silence for a moment.

“Since you’ve finally calmed down from last week, I think it’s only fair—”

“Look Brian, you caught me off guard. It was nothing, man. I know you have my back and you were just doing what you do best. Helping.”

“Yeah, I’ve never seen anyone get under your skin like Asa. You two looked like a married couple going at it.” Brian chuckled.

Simeon winced. He swirled the pale liquid around in his glass without looking at his brother.

"It appears that comment struck a nerve. Anyway, I think you need to know that she's serving in the dining room tonight."

Simeon shifted in his seat.

"Have you told her about the project yet?"

"No, I haven't talked to her since the rally."

"Why not. Why haven't you told her you might have an alternative site? I thought that was the whole idea."

Simeon took a long swallow from his glass. "How is everything here at the shelter?"

Brian walked around his desk and sat in the chair next to Simeon. He leaned forward resting his elbows on his knees. "I don't have a degree in psychology, but I talk to a lot of people here at the mission. I'm getting pretty good at reading between the lines."

Simeon took another swallow. "Don't try to diagnose me. What are you talking about?"

"It's Asa. I think you care about her."

"Mind your own business, Brian."

"You are my business, bro. I know you."

"Well maybe you're wrong this time."

The phone on his desk rang. Brian stared at him a long moment before moving to his desk and reaching for it.

While Brian shuffled through some papers on his desk, Simeon drained his glass. Brian pulled open a file cabinet and searched for something.

Simeon slipped out of the office and closed the door.

The clatter of plates and flatware echoed from the dining room. He made his way down the hall. From the dim light of the corridor, he spotted Asa talking with a group of men. Sweltering warmth raced across his body, settling under his collar. He tugged at his tie. One of the patrons unfolded a piece of paper then handed it to her. She pinned her hair behind her ear before taking the note in her delicate hand then reading it aloud. The genuine smile on her face lit up the room. She took a seat in front of the man before whispering something that made him flash a toothless grin. Afterwards she gave his hand a reassuring pat.

An image of Simeon's mother blurred his view. She had the same easy way with people. Simeon's chest tightened. The ache blanketing him since storming away from the rally grew heavier, bearing down on him like death. His heart pounded against the confines of his chest. He stepped into the dining room, blocking her way to the kitchen. The need to talk to her outweighed everything.

"Ah!" She yelped.

"I didn't mean to startle you."

"I guess I'm not allowed in the mission now, is that it?" She balanced a tray of soiled dishes.

"How have you been, Asa?" He took the tray from her.

Her mouth softened, she licked her lips but didn't respond.

"I see Brian talked you into helping out here. He can be pretty persuasive. My mother used to volunteer here, too."

"Brian has been very helpful. It didn't take much to

convince me to come. I've gotten more from being here than the people eating the meal." She turned around and tilted her head toward her sister. "I think Dakota is enjoying herself, too."

"Yes, it feels good to do something for others. I'm coming back next week," Dakota said as she caught up to her sister.

Simeon pushed the kitchen door open to allow them to walk ahead of him.

"I think you can call it a night, ladies. Good job." Miss Kitty wiped down the huge stainless steel stove.

"Can I talk with you, Asa?" Simeon asked.

"I'm riding with Dakota, so I need to be going."

"Uh, actually if you could get a ride home that would be great. Brian asked me out to dinner tonight and I'd--"

"I knew it," Asa squealed as she pulled her sister aside.

"Oh calm down. We're just having dinner, nothing to get excited about."

"How can you abandon me with the town ogre."

"You're a big girl. You can handle him." Dakota kissed her on the cheek before walking away.

I'm not sure I'm handling him or he's handling me.

Chapter Nineteen

Simeon adjusted his gait to walk beside Asa on the way to his car. Her arms hung at her sides and she kept her eyes on the sidewalk. He hated to admit being wrong, but maybe his behavior at the rally had been abrasive. Her delicate, ambrosial appearance didn't require such harsh words. He held the car door open and finally she met his gaze.

"Look, Asa—"

"No, you look, Simeon. You were out of order." Anger flashed in her eyes.

"Maybe so, but—"

She cut him off again. "I could have told you—"

"Yes you should have."

"What would you have done?" She placed her hand on the hood of the car.

"I've always been honest and up front with you, Asa. Whatever action I would have taken for the rally I would have shared with you."

She nodded and dropped her eyes. "You've made yourself very clear, your business comes before anything else. And now I need to do the same. I'm putting my needs before anything else. And I need to save the house I grew up in."

"I am what I am, Asa. You should know that by now."

She stared at him. "That is our problem. I don't really know you, Simeon. You're charming and considerate, but you're not the person I thought I knew."

"Who's fault is that? You moved away and married—"
He clamped his jaw.

"You didn't even know I existed," she shot back.
"What should I have done, keep hanging around
playgrounds until you noticed me?"

They were silent for a moment. Mission patrons filed
passed them as they exited the building. "Are you going to
let me drive you home?"

She looked at him, studied his face until her eyes came
to rest on his lips.

"I don't have any other choices." She took the
passenger seat. He walked around the car and slid behind
the wheel. The engine purred with a turn of the key.

When he merged onto the highway he put the windows
down. Her curls whipped across her face in the cool
evening air, hiding her eyes. He couldn't determine if she
still harbored any anger.

She reached for her purse, but placed it back on the
floor of the car without looking inside. Something outside
held her attention at a stop light, but the minute he took off
she started to fidget, again. An aura of tenderness
surrounded her. In all the years he'd known her, he never
saw her so vulnerable. Instead of the fiery, tenacious
woman that dogged his dreams, the woman seated beside
him emitted a sensitivity he didn't know she possessed.

Before making the right turn onto her block, he knew.
The certainty that they would be together for the rest of his
life was as powerful as his vision for the community
center. She slipped away once before. That wouldn't

happen again.

He slowed down and searched both sides of the street for a parking space near her house. After his second trip around the block, he double-parked in front of her house.

"My neighbor across the street is having a going away party tonight. You can let me out here."

"I'll let you out here and park down the street. I want to talk with you tonight, so I'll come back."

"I don't think there's a lot for you to say. You made your position clear at the rally. I get it, Simeon, you're tough. You play to win."

"There's a car behind me, let me park the car."

"That's fine." Asa stepped out.

He pulled into a space near the corner. If she was still angry maybe this should wait. But he couldn't ignore the gnawing in his stomach. It was time to face his feelings for her.

He hurried toward her house. His long strides covered the distance quickly. Simeon shifted his position, but still collided with a man headed toward him with his head down.

"Excuse me, man," the stranger said when he bumped into Simeon.

"Not a problem." Simeon watched the hooded man hurry around the corner.

Asa opened the door before he rang the bell. She'd changed into a tank top and a pair of shorts, her hair arranged into a knot which exposed her full face.

"I had to park a block away." He stepped into the hall. Scruffy charged at him. He sniffed his shoes while his tail wagged uncontrollably. "I think he's happy to see me."

"What does he know?" Asa lead the way to the living room and plopped down on the sofa. The room was only a little brighter than the last time he was here. "I haven't told him you're worse than the dog catcher, yet."

He removed his tie and shoved it into his breast pocket. She crossed her slender legs, but never looked away as he got comfortable. "Is it always going to be this way between us?"

She parted her lips, but clamped them before responding. Instead, she stared at him while Scruffy sat in her lap.

"I'm sorry for my behavior." He hoped his sincerity came through in his voice.

"I thought you would try to squelch the rally if you knew what I was planning."

"Maybe I would have tried to talk you out of doing something so public."

"And you may have been successful. That's why I didn't tell you."

Scruffy jumped down, his claws tapped the floor as he trotted out of the room. Asa folded her hands in her empty lap. Sadness lurked behind her eyes.

"Can we call a truce? We've known each other since grade school; we went to high school together and tormented each other along the way." He paused then said, "What do you say?"

"I hope that's not the most compelling argument you can make." The corners of her mouth stretched into a smile. "But you're right. Truce." She held out her hand for him. Instead of shaking it, he pulled her into his arms. His lips covered her soft mouth.

He'd missed touching her, tasting her, being with her. The desire that clutched him was almost crippling. He tightened his hold on her and plunged his tongue deeper into her mouth. She responded with a soft moan.

"Simeon, you're squeezing me a little too—"

He released her. "I'm sorry."

"I've missed you, Asa."

She ran her hand along his jaw and brushed her lips against his cheek. She glanced around the room. "Where's Scruffy?"

"He left the room a moment ago."

"He must need to go outside. He's probably scratching at the back door." She headed toward the kitchen. "I'll be right back."

Simeon stood up and stretched his arms above his head. He looked out the window, the street was empty now. Most of the houses were dark. He had Asa all to himself, minus the dog. Inviting her to the beach tomorrow would give him a chance to tell her about the project. Maybe they could concentrate on being nice to each other. Or even better, they could continue what they started at his house. Every night when his head hit the pillow, Asa populated his dreams. One night of her wasn't enough. He wanted more.

"Stop it!" Asa's shout rang through the house. There was fear in her voice.

Simeon turned sharply, startled. His spine stiffened. The deep constant growls from Scruffy pierced the air. He tore out of the living room, knocking over the coffee table in his haste. Asa loved that dog. There was no way she'd talked to him in that tone.

His eyes scanned the kitchen, adjusting to the bright light. "What the hell--"

The hooded stranger that he saw earlier gripped Asa by the wrists. Tears rolled down her face. Simeon's chest heaved for air. He balanced on the balls of his feet. His fists clenched. The tendons of his hands rippled against the skin. The kitchen table, chairs and the dog, all stood between him and Asa.

"What the hell are you doing? Let her go."

"Look man, this ain't any of your business. You better step--"

The fear in her eyes jerked him into action. "Let her arm go." Simeon's voice boomed in the room as he charged at Asa. He crossed the room so fast his feet barely made contact with the floor. He towered over the lanky stranger by several inches. Without hesitating, he grabbed the stranger's arm and twisted the twig high behind his back while wrapping his other arm around the thug's throat. He dragged him across the room away from Asa.

"Are you okay, Asa?" he asked once there was some distance between her and the intruder.

"Look man, this is between husband and wife. You

need to leave us alone. Who the hell are you anyway?"

"I'm not your wife!" Asa shouted while rubbing her wrist.

"Do you know this man? Is this true?"

"He's my ex-husband. Ex-husband, Eric. Get that though your head." She spat out the words. "You have no business being here. I made that perfectly clear. There is nothing you can say that will change my mind. The divorce has been final for two years. Go back to Atlanta to whoever is keeping your bed warm these days."

"Asa, I'm different now. Give me another chance. You know you can't walk away from me like that."

"I can and I did."

"Tell me what you want me to do, Asa." Simeon tightened his hold. He could snap the intruder's arm with a simple tug. "Do you want me to call the police?"

"I want him out of here. Forever." Anger flashed in her dark eyes.

"Look, Asa, don't call the cops. I'll leave."

Her eyes darted from Eric to Simeon then came to rest on the dog.

"It's your call, Asa," Simeon said.

"No...no police. Just get him out of here."

"You heard her, man. It's over. Don't show up around here again." Simeon released his neck and opened the kitchen door. He held Eric's arm until they were on the back porch.

"Get the hell off me, man," Eric jerked away when Simeon loosened his grip "What are you, her bodyguard?"

"I'm whatever she needs."

"Well, I ain't begging her no more." He ran down the steps.

"You can tell her if she changes her mind, I don't want her back. I'm done with her."

Simeon kept his eyes on Eric until he disappeared into the darkness, before going back inside.

Asa stood at the kitchen sink, running water over the dishes. Tears streamed down her face.

"Are you all right?" He placed his hands on her shoulder. She nodded. "He's gone, Asa. He's not coming back."

"Eric is like a bad penny, he keeps showing up."

"Are you afraid of him?"

She held a plate under the running facet. "Not until tonight. He pushed his way through the door when I opened it for the dog. The way he grabbed my--" She extended her arms. Red marks peppered her wrists. She placed the plate in the dishwasher with a heavy sigh.

Running water was the only sound in the kitchen for several moments. Asa stared into the soapy water as she rinsed another plate.

"Do you think I should have called the police?"

"I don't know. It looks like he might have gotten the message. I can stay here tonight if you want."

"I-I can't ask you to do that. You can't keep rescuing

me. You and I—”

“You didn’t ask me. I offered.”

She turned around, her eyes sparked with more tears. “Would you? Just for the night.”

He pulled her away from the sink, into his arms. She trembled with such force, her earrings clanged. He reassured her. “I’ll be here for as many nights as you need me.”

He continued to hold her, listening to her breathe. Seconds turned into minutes. Gradually the tension left her body and her earrings stopped moving.

“Suppose I need you for a week?” she finally said.

“Then I’ll be here.”

“Suppose I say a month?”

“Don’t you get it, Asa? I’ll be here for as long as you need me.”

She pulled back and looked into his eyes. “What are you saying, Simeon?”

He reached across her to turn off the water. She continued to look into his eyes, but he couldn’t answer her question. His tongue found her tongue. Nothing else mattered right now.

§ § §

For just a moment, she allowed his words to penetrate her heart. Reading more into his statement would only mean hurt later. She wallowed in the glow of his statement for as long as it took them to walk back to the living room. Then just as quickly, she pushed aside his reassuring words. This wasn't a fantasy and Simeon wasn't about to sweep her off her feet and carry her to the castle.

She dropped onto the sofa and continued to rub her wrist. "Will Eric leave me alone?"

"I'll stick around for a few days to be sure." He sat beside her.

"Just tonight. After tonight, I'll be fine." He ran his hand over his belt buckle; she followed the movement. "I don't need a protector. I can take care of myself."

"Nobody knows that better than me." Scruffy ran into the room and jumped into her lap. They sat in silence while she stroked the dog. She could pretend to be tough as nails for as long as it took to believe it. It was time for her to take care of herself.

"It seems like we keep getting in each other's way. We keep doing some kind of dance, I'm not sure if it's a war dance or a love dance." She searched his face for a response.

He dropped his head. "One of these days we'll take time to define it."

"What did you mean? Back there in the kitchen when you said..."

He stretched his legs. "I'm here for you. I want you to know that."

She wanted to hear more. Scruffy was here for her too, but she wanted more than companionship. She wanted him to touch her, for a lifetime, forever, and even longer than that. She wanted to feel his skin against her skin, his breath against her neck.

She grabbed his hand and pulled him toward her. She placed her mouth over his, straddled his lap, and tilted her head to deepen the kiss. His tongue nudged hers with such fury she forgot to breathe. The warmth from his body was like a furnace; her body began to tingle. Lust burned in her loins, rose up her back, along her spine, slow and steady. He slipped his hands under her tank top and stroked her breasts, while his tongue continued to devour her. He rolled her nipples between his thumbs and fingers, the sensation filling her beyond constraint. She pulled her top over her head, exposing her breasts to the moonlight that came through the window. The smartest thing to do was to send Simeon away, but she didn't want to be strong tonight.

"Aren't you concerned about your neighbors?" He nodded at the windows.

"Believe me, no one can see over that hedge or around that tree."

"Should I be concerned that you know this?"

She shook her head and reached for his belt buckle. After freeing the narrow strip of leather she unbuttoned his shirt and caressed his chest. His hard abs constricted under her hands. Her breathing became sporadic as she kissed his forehead before crushing her mouth against his.

When she released his mouth he held her at a distance and searched her face.

"Asa?" Uncertainty flashed in his eyes.

"Yes. Yes Simeon, I'm sure." She pulled off her shorts and thong in one fluid motion and stood naked in front of him.

He caressed her thighs and then cupped her buttocks. His tongue traced a circle around her navel, then across her stomach. The warmth of his touch sent her emotions skyrocketing. He pulled off shoes, socks, and pants. His hands kneaded her thighs. The heat of his touch ignited her core. She groaned. His tongue found its way to her left nipple and drew on it. His suckling intensified; her nipples throbbed.

He pulled back, allowing his eyes to run the length of her body. He brushed his hands across her nipples. Pleasure danced up her spine, making her knees wobble. She parted her lips slightly and he found her tongue. Stroking and taunting her tongue simultaneously.

Maybe she wanted too much. Love. Maybe she should be content just being with him. Her body craved him like flowers craved sunshine. She could no more let him go than she could forget to breathe. Blood rushed to her engorged nub, pulsating like miniature earthquakes. She rocked her hips in response to his touch. The exquisite feeling left her breathless; she released his tongue to catch her breath.

Her orgasm began with a small tremor and grew with each stroke of his hand. She wanted him inside of her, to fill the emptiness she'd ignored for so long.

He retrieved a condom from his pants pocket and rolled it into place. With his leg stretched in front of him, she straddled him again, facing his feet. She came down on his penis with a slowness that made him groan with pleasure. The thick feel of his shaft filled her like hot steel. She tightened her muscles around his penis, claiming the erection that throbbed inside of her. She slid up and down with such precision, each thrust drove him deeper into her folds leaving her seething with desire. He held on to her hips, her fingers dug into his thighs. Her desire for him was so intense she struggled to control her momentum. She increased her movement, her head thrown back as she muffled the cry growing in her throat. Her muscles contracted, pulsing against his penis. He gripped her hips, slowed her down as his body tensed and jerked. Together their bodies pulsated. She clasped onto him. His hands coiled around her waist, pressing his damp chest to her back.

"Is this how you plan to protect me? Who will protect me against you?"

"You may look delicate and dainty, but...but woman you are a handful." His lusty voice whispered in her ear as he pulled out of her.

"That's good, right?" she asked over her shoulder.

"It's very good."

She felt his penis jerk to life against her thigh. With care, he shifted on the small sofa until she was beneath him. He placed his mouth over hers, his kiss slow and tender.

Getting lost in her emotions was so easy. Every cell in her body screamed for him. She couldn't pull away.

This time he was in control. He found the base of her

neck and ran his tongue along her collarbone before kissing the tender, soft skin. She released a low moan and began to rotate her hips. He whispered her name. The husky sound of his voice was enough to drive her to orgasm again, but she refused to succumb.

He slipped his finger into the soft, wet folds of her core, found her nub and stroked it gently. Nothing had ever felt so exquisite. Heat ricocheted across her flesh. He found that sensitive spot and seized it until she gasped with ecstasy.

"Simeon, please--" With her plea he removed his finger and slid into her. She arched her back, drawing him in deeper. Her hands raced across his massive shoulders. Her hips bucked; he kissed her earlobe before whispering her name again and joining her.

I love him. I love Simeon.

Chapter Twenty

The slight bruises on her wrists brought the memory of Eric's crushing grip rushing back. Asa reached across the bed for Simeon, but the space next to her was empty. Her eyes flew open. She was alone. Dread flared in her stomach as she bolted upright. In spite of her independent drive she wished Simeon had stayed a little longer. Stayed the night.

Panic raced across her flesh at the sound of footsteps on the hardwood floor. She drew the sheet over her breasts as she scrunched low in the bed pushing against the headboard and scanned the room for her cell phone.

Simeon pushed the door open with his foot. He carried two cups of tea. "It's about time you woke up." He winked at her.

"I thought you were gone," her voice cracked.

His forehead creased as he searched her face. He set both mugs on the nightstand. "Why'd you think that? You said you needed me to stay a month. And I plan to." He leaned over and brushed her lips, before inserting his tongue in her mouth. His breath tasted minty. A hint of stubble tickled her face.

A night of fire-hot sex, followed by tea in bed and, delivered by the sexiest man she knew could be addicting. She fell back against the pillow and ran her eyes over his exposed chest then up to his dark eyes. Something flashed there, something she'd never seen or noticed before, and it tugged at her heart. But just as quickly it disappeared.

Could he feel the same way about her that she felt about him?

"Take off your pants and come back to bed, please," she said. He obeyed, baring his muscular legs. After last night she should be satisfied for a month, but as he crawled over her a slow burn reignited between her thighs. The warmth from his body pressed against her. Her mantra was to stay focused on the important stuff, but it was getting harder to remember anything but his scent, his touch and the way he tasted.

She nuzzled her head into his chest. "Last night you said you wanted to talk. What about?"

He rose on one elbow while stroking her breasts. "What if I told you there may be a chance to save your house?"

She sprang back up. "What— How—"

He sat up against the headboard and grabbed her hands.

"Before you get excited let me explain. The deal is not complete yet. The Plaid Group agreed to look at another parcel of land."

"That's absolutely fabulous! You should have told me that the minute we got in your car last night."

His lips curled into a smile. "You weren't in the mood."

"I've hounded you for weeks. I've done everything except get down on my knees. Sometimes I think you like torturing me."

"We'll that's not true. You're just very persistent."

"My sisters think I'm nuts. I've even asked my realtor to find a condo for me. After the rally I just about gave up on the whole idea of keeping the house.”

“But please don’t get too excited yet.”

“Well, thank you for trying. I really mean that.” She kissed his full, luscious lips.

§ § §

Water beaded on his shoulders as Simeon sauntered across the bedroom, nude. His dark eyes danced with mischief as they raked over her. Starting at her eyes, he slowly moved to her mouth before devouring the rest of her body. Desire oozed from him. He ran his tongue over his lips and she knew she was in too deep to get away without being affected. She had sheltered her heart safely away, but Simeon found the key. If she didn’t slow down, she would fall hard.

His close-cropped hair glistened and his washboard stomach was still damp. She sucked her stomach in, suddenly feeling self-conscious of her softness.

“Take that towel off.” He tugged at the towel that covered her. “I like looking at your sexiness.”

“We’ve used all the condoms, so stop looking.” She pulled a thong from the drawer and slipped it on. “Let me cook you breakfast.”

“Take a ride with me.” He wrapped his arm around her waist.

“Before or after we eat?”

“Spend the weekend with me in Rehoboth. I need to go down today to open up the beach house.”

She faced him. "Beach house. You have a beach house? Who are you? How many houses does a single man need?"

"Come with me. I'll tell you all about the Simeon Harper you don't know." He chuckled. His eyes twinkled when he laughed.

She loved the sound of his laughter. "Is there more to tell? I've known you most of my life." He sat down on the bed and pulled her closer. The light kisses he planted on her stomach fueled her hunger and any affirmations about staying focus faded.

"Simeon, you were saying?"

"Oh yeah." He grinned. "No, you don't really know me. Pack some of this fancy stuff you wear and let's go." He picked up her sundress and twirled it around.

"Will you feed me?"

"I'll feed your stomach, and your soul, as much as you want. Every minute of every day."

§ § §

After a stop at Simeon's house to pick up clothes, he pulled onto Route 1 South along with the other beach-goers. Traffic bogged down at every toll plaza. The closer they got to the beaches the slower the traffic moved.

A weekend away from the city was an idea engraved in pleasure. Even if he didn't want commitment and she didn't want a fling she couldn't resist. She wanted something solid. She wanted a marriage like the one her parents shared. After Eric, it was something she never though she would want again, but being around Simeon, with him, made her heart yearn for the complete package.

"What do you have to do down here this weekend?" Asa rubbed the top of Scruffy's head as he sat at her feet.

"Spend time with you." He winked. "I'll make sure we have plenty of food for you two. But mostly I just want to make sure the house is ready for the season. Check that everything is working. You know, toilet flushing, water running, that sort of thing. And we'll get some rest. I need stamina to spend time with you."

She smiled. They road in silence for several minutes. The salty smell of the ocean filled the car as they neared the water. Pedestrian traffic increased with families heading to the beach with tightly rolled towels tucked under their arms and carrying coolers and beach chairs. Several bicyclists peddled on both sides of the road. From their leisurely pace, Asa knew it was time to calm her racing thoughts and relax.

A group of clapboard townhouses graced the bay side of the highway and larger stately window-filled houses dotted the ocean side. A visit to the Delaware beaches was always a treat from their father at the end of every school year. It felt good to be back in a place with so many pleasant memories.

She faced Simeon. "Let's get Fisher's caramel popcorn while we're here."

"You're a fan?"

"I love that stuff. It reminds me of summer and my

dad."

"Your dad, huh?"

Asa saw his jaw tighten. "You never talk about your father."

"Nope, I don't. There isn't a whole lot to talk about. He lived on a bench, drank too much and died young. End of story." Simeon pulled the car into a carport on the side of a three-story structure that faced the ocean. Each level boasted a balcony. The house looked massive with the horizon as its backdrop. A rooftop deck was nestled into one of the dormers.

As soon as Asa took off his leash, Scruffy charged to the water's edge. "Scruffy! Come back here." She kicked off her sandals to chase the dog across the warm sand. She wasn't fast enough to catch him before he plunged into the receding tide.

The shock of cold water on her feet made her squeal. "This water is freezing," she yelled over her shoulder.

"It doesn't get warm until late July or early August. I'll let you two play. I'm content to watch from here." Simeon stood on a sand dune.

"I'm not going back in there. My feet are freezing." Asa ran up the dune to stand next to Simeon. She stood close enough to feel his skin against hers.

Together they watched Scruffy try to catch a seagull. Simeon wrapped his arm around her shoulder. She let her body go limp against him. She wanted time to stand still long enough to imprint this image on her memory forever. Years of searching and fumbling had finally landed her where she needed to be. But Simeon wasn't ready for a commitment. His business was his only long-term relationship.

Listening to her parents could have saved her some disappointment. Years ago, maybe she and Simeon could have carved out a future together. Was it too late for them? What were they doing? Where would this relationship end up? She wanted to believe he felt something for her, loved her. But, she was afraid to want too much.

"How soon will we know for certain?" she asked.

"About your house? It shouldn't take too long. I'm hoping to know something by the end of the week." He tightened his hold on her.

"Thank you, Simeon." She turned in his arms and stood on her toes to kiss him. His mouth was warm. The sound of the waves along with a few squawks from the seagulls and Scruffy's barking were the only noises. She encircled his waist. Her heart swelled as he accepted her kiss.

The dog staggered out of the water, his tongue hung with exhaustion. He ran toward her.

"Aack," Asa yelled when he shook his whole body and sprayed them with water.

"Since he's wet should we dry him off before going inside?" Asa asked. Simeon reached for her hand as they walked to the house.

He unlocked the door. "There's no carpet on the ground level, so he's fine. I'll get a towel and dry him off." He held the door open and allowed her and the dog to enter. "Go on upstairs to the living room; I'll be up as soon as I dry him off."

She kicked off her shoes and padded barefoot up the stairs. Without waiting for permission she pulled the floor to ceiling shutters open to expose the view. Glaring sunshine flooded the room and bounced off the glass surface of the water. The heat of the sun warmed her face.

The spectacular room, this place looked much friendlier than his family room in Bristol. Personal touches of Simeon littered the cozy room, a family portrait on the end table, several football trophies adorned the case in the corner, a book along with a CD lay on the sandy colored sofa. It looked like he walked away a moment ago, instead of months ago.

Scruffy ran up the stairs ahead of Simeon. "I love this room. With this view how do you ever tear yourself away to go back to Bristol?"

"It's easier than you think when you have a business to run... and you're alone."

Asa sat on a bar stool next to Simeon. "I'll bite. Tell me why a good looking, wealthy man is all alone."

He turned to look out the window. Instead of answering, he stood up.

"I'm going to the car to get our bags and the food. I promised to feed you and Scruffy tonight."

§ § §

Is she toying with me? Was that last question meant to taunt me? Simeon descended the stairs two at a time and pushed open the door. Outside he ran his hands over his head. He needed fresh air. This wasn't difficult; he knew how to keep his emotions in check. But the way she said his name or looked at him, everything about her bypassed his head and went straight to his heart. He exhaled slowly.

Only one person knew his secrets, and his mother was gone. She was the only woman he openly admitting to loving. Asa almost tugged that confession out of him again. He couldn't lay himself open like that. If the new parcel of land didn't work Asa could turn on him. If she knew a wrecking ball could knock down her house in a matter of weeks she might scurry back into a hole that he could never coax her out of.

He pulled their bags from the trunk along with the food they had purchased. "Check yourself, brother, before you end up sorry and pathetic like your father," he muttered under his breath as he juggled bags and headed inside.

She stood on the balcony looking at the ocean. Instead of disturbing her, he put the food and bags away. Maybe by the time she came back inside, she wouldn't be looking for answers to probing questions.

§ § §

A while later, he massaged herbs into the chicken breasts before spreading them with fontina cheese and basil. He tied each breast closed with twine then placed them in the oven.

"Dinner should be ready in an hour," he yelled.

Asa lay curled up on the sofa. After a long walk on the

beach and the caramel popcorn, she looked exhausted. Even the dog looked worn out, sprawled next to her on the floor. Asa's eyelids struggled to remain open. He would never tire of this view. He imagined a long, grueling day eased by coming home to see her brilliant smile.

After several moments, he shook himself and released the image. "You aren't too tired to eat, are you?"

"No. I'm just enjoying myself. I haven't felt this relaxed since I came back home." She stretched her arms over her head.

The swell of her breasts peaked over her v-neck top. Every time he looked at her, his body reacted. Instead of going to lay with her on the couch and taking her soft, lush body, he plucked two glasses from the cabinet. He selected a bottle of Riesling from the wine refrigerator.

"Come with me; let's sit outside until dinner is ready." He opened the French doors and led the way down the stairs to the lanai. He placed the tray on the table before lighting the outside fire pit. The glow from the ceramic briquettes threw just enough light as the sun settled low on the horizon. The ocean barely made a sound as it brushed the shore.

He sat next to Asa on the double-wide lounge chair. In all the years he had owned this house, she was his first visitor. He had it decorated with her in mind, but back then it was only a wish, something he had hoped for, without promise.

He poured a glass of wine for her. They sat in silence for several minutes as the sun faded out of sight.

"This is nice, Simeon."

"I've kept my promise then? I've fed you breakfast and lunch and in a few minutes dinner."

"You've kept your promise," she assured him before snuggling against him. She reached for his hand. "So the only reason you ignored me in high school is because you thought we lived on opposite sides of the tracks? That's why you continually ignored me?"

"High school, huh? Are you sure you want to go all the way back to then?"

"Do you ever answer any questions or is being evasive something they teach you in business school?"

"Maybe you ask too many questions?" He nudged her.

"See, you're doing it again. You didn't answer my question. I want an answer. I've always wondered. I thought it was just poor timing or something like that."

"It was poor timing. My family had some malfunctions that were quite consuming. I could only think about the basics; food and shelter. And if you remember how I dressed back then, I didn't think too much about clothes."

Asa's eyes were riveted on him. "I had no idea—"

"That was my intention. I didn't want anyone to know." He shifted

"So, you weren't just a mean teenager?"

"I haven't got a mean bone in my body. Want to see?" He pulled her into his lap.

Especially when it comes to you.

Chapter Twenty-One

Asa moaned as she woke up. "Turn back the clock. It can't be Sunday morning already."

Simeon placed a pillow over his head. "I usually come here to get some rest, to get away from the rat race in Bristol. You didn't let me rest this weekend. I think I'm more exhausted now than before I left."

"You think that's my fault? I didn't keep you up all night, you kept me up."

"You're the hot one. I can't keep my hands off of you." He sat up in the bed.

His eyes were locked on her. Some unspoken emotion hid behind his hooded lids. She'd prodded him with enough questions this weekend to have the answers she needed, but he'd sidestepped enough of them to let her know to leave it alone. His evasiveness did nothing to quiet her growing attraction to him. Her chest pounded, she couldn't turn away from the surge of emotions swelling in the pit of her stomach.

"Simeon, I love you," she whispered. His flinch happened so quickly she wondered if she'd imagined it. She waited for him to reply, to acknowledge that he at least heard her. Instead, he continued searching her face. He dropped onto his elbows, placing his full weight on top of her. His tongue parted her lips, his movements were slow and concentrated, just like the look he gave her. He released her tongue and bit softly on her bottom lip before rolling out of bed.

"I think you just like my cooking," he called over his

shoulder as he made his way to the bathroom.

She closed her eyes so tight a burst of color flashed behind her lids. The bathroom door closed with a thud.

"Shit, shit, shit." She punched the pillow. *Did I really say I loved him?* Those words weren't supposed to slip past her tongue unless she was talking to Scruffy. She looked over the side of the bed to find the dog sprawled out on the floor. She reached down to rub the top of his head

"I can't stay out of trouble," she whispered. He wagged his tail. "Shit," she uttered again. After pulling on a pair of shorts and a T-shirt she yelled to Simeon, "I'll go downstairs and start breakfast."

"Don't bother. We'll grab something quick before getting on the highway."

Quick? That certainly isn't a good sign.

Asa put the window down in the car. A humid rush of air blew through the car but did little to cool her. The noise made it difficult to have a conversation. She glimpsed Simeon out of the corner of her eye. His clenched jaw pulsed with tension. Could her emotional confession have instigated that strain? How could she have slipped like that? All that talk about enjoying the single life vanished after one lustful weekend. But it slipped out. She half expected him to tell her he loved her, too. That's what she wanted. This weekend, he acted like she was important to him. The cooking, the pampering, the lovemaking. Or was it just sex? Maybe it was all part of his charm, part of his single life.

She watched the scenery out the window, her hands pressed in her lap.

"Are you okay? You're really quiet." Simeon shifted gears and changed lanes.

"Yeah, yeah. I'm fine." She pulled down the sun visor and flipped open the mirror. "I'm just wondering how I'm going to hide these bags under my eyes. I'm supposed to go to New York again on Monday morning to meet with folks from Mercedes Benz about the fashion show. They want their designers to look as fresh as their clothing lines."

"Like I said earlier, it's not my fault." He grinned. "I know we ate a hurried breakfast in the car, so do you want to stop and get something to eat before I drop you off?"

The weekend, the conversation, and that flinch all needed close examination. To scrutinize each detail required space between them. The restrictive area in the car wasn't enough room to regroup her emotions.

"No, I think I need to call it a day. Besides, what would we do with Scruffy while we're eating? It's too hot for him to stay in the car."

"Did you enjoy your breakfast?"

She rubbed her stomach that protruded slightly over her drawstring shorts.

"You did a great job, my stomach can testify to that." She shifted in her seat to dislodge the twinge of disappointment that crept up her spine. When Simeon pulled in front of the house Asa climbed from the car. The dog jumped out behind her. Simeon followed them into the house and placed her bag at the foot of the stairs.

"Are you sure you don't want me to stay tonight?"

"Yes, I'm sure. It's been two nights; Eric is probably back with one of his old loves by now.

"Can we have dinner tonight?" He pulled her into his arms.

"I'm leaving for New York in the morning. I need to prepare for my meetings." She peered into his eyes. "Tell me something, Simeon." She slipped out of his embrace to see his eyes. "What are we doing here?"

His chin shot up. He shoved his hands in his pocket. "We...I thought we were just enjoying each other's company."

"Is that all it was for you?" She shifted her position to see his eyes.

"You're very special to me, Asa. More special than any woman has ever been." He held her face between his hands. The warmth from his palms heating her face. He kissed her lips tenderly before pushing his tongue deeper into her mouth.

After a minute she released his mouth. She nodded. Being special wouldn't be enough.

§ § §

Tension congregated in Simeon's neck. A decision about the mall was due today. His gut told him the news wasn't good. A flurry of phone calls this week indicated Golden Leaf remained on the chopping block.

Simeon rubbed his thumb over the crystal of his watch. He pictured Asa at the beach house. Remembering images of her curled up on the couch, stretched out on the lounge and next to him in bed, and none of it was enough. She was due back from New York and he couldn't wait to see her.

He could call her now. She had to be home and settled in. He wanted to go to New York with her, but a packed schedule kept him in the office. Besides, he wanted to stay close to see and hear the daily reviews. In the beginning, it looked like an easy switch, but after further investigation, several problems cropped up with both of his major projects.

He glanced at his watch again. Brad should have called by now with the results.

"Catherine, give Stevens a call and tell him I want those final results today, before I leave the office."

Catherine stood in his door with a pad in her hand. She scribbled a note. "Anything else?"

"Yeah. Send three dozen red long stem roses to Asa. I want the card to say, Congratulations on your success."

"Got it."

He picked up the phone and dialed Asa's number. "How was your trip?"

"I'm exhausted, but the trip was great. I saw the venue for the show. We discussed my line." The warmth of her voice eased the tension in his shoulders. "The praise was enough to keep me afloat for a week. I missed you, though."

"I missed you, too. I—" He clamped down on his bottom lip. He almost said the unthinkable. "I can't wait to get you in bed." He reared back in his chair to place his feet on the desk.

"We talked every day; sometimes even more."

"It's not the same. I can't kiss or hold a phone."

"I could have sworn we had phone sex one night."

"Yes, I know I did. And I'm here to tell you it wasn't anything like the real thing. What time can I see you? I want the real thing."

"I'm having dinner with my sister tonight. Come by later; by the time you show up she'll be long gone. Any word yet on the project? It's been over a week."

"I'll call again later today." He tried to keep the concern out of his voice.

"Why is it taking so long?"

"Let's talk tonight when I get there." After they said good-bye, Simeon placed the phone in the cradle. He saved the document he was working on and shut down his computer. He spun his chair to face the picture of his mother on the credenza. Her gentle smile warmed him. The pain evident in her eyes spoke for her. She wanted to do more for her children, for her family. Every day produced a new struggle for her to overcome. Today she would be proud. The vision the two of them hatched together while trying to stay warm in the city housing project inched closer to reality. Other than his brother, no one else cared that the Harper family had finally turned that corner.

He squared his shoulders. Rain peppered his window making it hard to see the city skyline. Below on the street, brightly colored umbrellas hurried from one spot to the next. He picked up the phone and punched in Brad's number.

"Brad, where are we on the study?"

"I think I have good news."

"Let's hear what you found."

"Moving the strip mall is a no-brainer. The new location is even better than the Golden Leaf location. It has easy access to the west side of town. The population in that area is denser. But—"

"Finish up Brad, I don't have all day." Simeon fisted his hands.

"The final result just arrived on my desk. The community center needs more parking than the parcel can accommodate. The only plan that makes sense is to move the community center to the Golden Leaf parcel. It's the perfect location if we move the strip mall."

"That wasn't part of the proposal." Simeon ran his hand across his face. The tension in his neck spread across his shoulders.

"I know, but if we have to search for other acreage for the community center we may have to delay the project for a few years."

"That's not an option," he insisted.

"It's your decision. The crews are ready."

"You're sure about the results? There're no other

options?"

"I double checked. I even called city planning to confirm the requirements."

"Let's get together tomorrow to go over the details." Simeon ended the call.

He stretched his jaw, releasing his rear teeth from the repeated grinding. His slow gait to the door didn't help sort out his thoughts. With his hands clasped behind him, he strolled back across his office to peer out the window. The rain had turned into a fine drizzle. Steam rose off the hot pavement.

Telling Asa this news would be difficult. She was the roadblock that could make him forsake the dream that gave his mother a reason to keep going when cancer consumed her. He shook his head. He had to keep his promise to his mother. She deserved this one wish even if she hadn't lived to see it.

The phone rang. He saw his brother's name on the caller ID. "Brian, how are you?"

"Sim, I haven't seen you since you left the shelter with my volunteer. How've you been?" His brother chuckled.

"Asa hasn't kicked me to the curb yet, if that's what you mean."

"Good to hear that," said Brian

"Are you free tonight? Can we get together for dinner?"

"Can't tonight. I'm short on help here tonight. But come on down, I could use an extra pair of hands."

"I was hoping we could talk," Simeon said.

"We'll talk. See you shortly." Simeon hung up the phone. Brian never changed. With his brother he could let his guard down.

Less than an hour later, the persistent drizzle annoyed him as it distorted his view through the car window. Every few seconds the windshield wipers cleared the window as he made his way to the shelter. He pulled into the back lot and parked.

"Hey, it's about time you got here," Brian yelled as Simeon entered the shelter kitchen. "Wash your hands and grab an apron off the hook. I need someone to help me serve dinner. A couple of volunteers canceled on me tonight."

Simeon walked to the back of the kitchen and prepared to help. He sniffed the air. Something smelled good. He spotted the source of the familiar aroma. Across the room a cook sliced meatloaf and buried it in thick brown gravy. The smell reminded Simeon of one Christmas long ago, when his family was together and happy. He pushed the memory out of his mind as he walked into the dining room.

§ § §

"I should have known you'd put me to work," Simeon said at the end of the night.

"You know you love it." Brian pulled two cans of ginger ale from the refrigerator. "Have a soda," he said before sitting down. "So what's new with my baby brother?" Brian placed the can to his mouth and took a long swallow.

"Nothing's ever static in the development business. Today it's good news and bad news. The community center moves forward. Unfortunately it's going up at Golden Leaf." He rolled the can between his palms.

Neither said anything for several moments. The large industrial wall clock ticked off the seconds.

"Mom would be proud of you, Sim. You did it. I knew you would. So, how does Asa feel about the demolition?"

"I haven't told her the plans for her house fell through."

"What are you waiting on?" Simeon took a big swallow from the soda can. "I guess that's one thing I inherited from our father. I'm no good at relationships either, and I've taken procrastination to a whole new level."

"You know that's just an excuse, don't you?" Brian raised a brow. "One of these days you and I are going to have to look that devil in the eye. Stare down that fear. Just because Mom and Dad were so miserable doesn't mean we'll turn out like them."

"Name one happily married couple? If you've got all the answers then why aren't you in a relationship?"

"Well, it's not because I'm afraid." He nudged his brother's shoulder. "You care about her. I can tell by the way you look at her. A few weeks ago you came in here, shoulders slumped, looking defeated. You saw Asa in the dining room and the next thing I know you're escorting her out of here grinning like you found a pot of gold."

Simeon shifted in his seat. He drained the soda can before responding. "I can't put my feelings for her ahead of the people waiting for a decent place to live. I'm seeing her later tonight; after I tell her I think that'll be the end."

"You know that's not true. Give her a chance. Maybe you won't have to break it off."

"It's not important."

"I think it is, Sim." Brian put his soda down. "Look, I see men every day that ignore their feelings and end up with some hard knocks. I know that won't happen to you, but it never does anyone any good to suppress their feelings. Talk to her, tell her how you feel. It's sure got to beat hanging out here. Pride never warmed a bed."

But with Asa I have no control.

Chapter Twenty-Two

Asa licked her fingers. Sweet peach juice ran down her wrist. Her heart billowed with joy. Two hundred hits on her website, eight new orders, and no major meltdown with the house from the last big rainstorm were all good signs. Every magical minute with Simeon only enhanced her bliss. Even though he hadn't expressed any feelings for her, his touch, his kisses added to her euphoria.

Nothing with him came easy. One day she would have to let him go; the thought settled in her stomach like a rock. She held the counter until the feeling passed. Until then she planned to enjoy every minute. For now, everything was perfect. Hearing him whisper her name caused tremors to run along her flesh. His touch kindled a fire in her that burned slow and steady until he carried her to release.

"What are you grinning about?" asked Dakota.

Asa looked up and concentrated on her sister. "Nothing. I was just thinking about the show." She put the pie in the oven then joined her sister at the counter.

"What do you think?" Asa asked.

"I love the color palette for this collection. These greens and blues are so rich." Dakota fingered the Italian wool crepe dress. Asa nodded as Dakota picked up the gown. "This is gorgeous." Dakota held the grand finale gown against her body. "I want you to make me one. Not that I'll have anywhere to wear it. Just having this gown in my closet will make me feel better. I'll get tickets to an awards program in New York. We can wear our 'Asa

Designs' down the red carpet." She laughed.

"I think that calls for a toast." Asa raised her wine glass.

"I'm proud of you, Asa. You came back. You knew what you wanted and went after it. Including Simeon," Dakota smirked.

"Well, I'm not so sure I'd count Simeon as one of my successes. We're just enjoying each other's company for now. We're not serious, no commitment." Asa turned away from her sister. Being away from him for a week magnified the gap between them. "Dakota, how was your dinner with Brian?"

"Don't start with me, Asa. It was just dinner. Save me any sermons."

"Fine. I won't say a word." Asa crossed her arms under her breasts. "Let's eat while we're waiting on the pie. I'm hungry."

"Pie and lasagna, now that's a meal that would make Mom cringe." Dakota sipped her wine.

"I decided to cook my favorites. I started to make a big dish of macaroni and cheese too. But my thighs are getting thick and I didn't need all that pasta." Asa grimaced. "Thank you for celebrating with me. Simeon is working to save the house; the shop opens in a month. I've hired an assistant." Asa raised her glass again.

"Here, here." Dakota tipped her glass toward her sister's. "So it's final...the house isn't being torn down?"

"Well, it's not for certain," Asa hesitated. "But Simeon believes the other parcel of land will work for the mall."

"What if it doesn't?"

"Then I'll move. As much as I love this place it's..." Asa hesitated.

"Oh, boy." Dakota dropped her head in the palm of her hand.

Asa placed a large piping hot square of lasagna on the center of the plate and handed it to her sister.

"Oh, Dakota, relax. I'm a big girl. If it doesn't work out, I'll be fine. I promise I won't break down and cry in my soup." She shrugged her shoulder. "It's just this house is filled with happy memories."

"Are you kidding me? Happy times?" Dakota raised her brow.

"Yeah, why?" Asa focused her attention on her sister.

"Never mind. Just forget it."

"What? What is it?" Dakota frowned. "What are you keeping from me?" Asa asked.

"It's just that I have different memories of this house, that's all."

"Like what?"

"First, it's those block parties you thought were so great. We were always begging other people to bring food. We couldn't throw the party on our own. I thought it was embarrassing and so did Dad."

"Back then neighbors came together and helped each other. That was the best part of the whole day."

"Well, Mim and Pepa may have thought so, but Dad

sure hated it. He and Mom argued about them all the time," Dakota said.

"That's not true."

"He called the house a money pit," Dakota continued. "That last summer he finally convinced Mom to put it on the market."

"To sell it? But why?" The room was quiet for a moment. Asa's skin began to tingle. "What?"

"They were talking about divorce."

Asa clasped her hands at her chest. "Oh, Dakota, you're suspicious of everything. Mom and Dad would never get a divorce. They loved each other."

Dakota cleared her throat. "It's true."

Asa searched the small kitchen, looking for something solid to focus on. She saw the cookie jar with the painted brown gingerbread man that smiled back at her. She refused to look at her sister until her breathing slowed. "But what about Mim? Where..."

Dakota stood behind her. She rubbed Asa shoulders as if the massage would make the words more palatable. "Mim was going to move with Mom. They didn't want to worry you since you were in school. Mom knew your marriage was in trouble. She didn't want to tell you until she knew for certain what they were going to do."

Asa couldn't form any words. She picked up the fork. The sterling silver was heavy in her palm. It fell to the table with a loud thud. Her stomach tightened as she slumped against the back of the chair and shifted her gaze. This couldn't be true. How could something this important be happening in her family without her knowledge?

She pushed her plate away. "Why didn't anyone tell me? Didn't you think it was important for me to know? Even when I came back for the funeral, you could have said something then."

"What would have been the use? They died before making a final decision. No one will ever know if they were able to patch up their relationship or not. It was easier to mourn them believing they were happy together and still in love. You know how Pepa and Mim were. They never talked about unhappy or unpleasant things."

"But this was too important to sugar coat. I feel like I've been living with a different family for the last several years, thinking my marriage caused the friction between me and Mom. Maybe it wasn't. Maybe her comments and reaction were more to do with her marriage, not mine. How many other secrets are just waiting to be dug up around here?" Asa glared at her sister.

Dakota placed her plate in the sink. "Mom was never angry at you for marrying. She just didn't want you to make the same mistakes she made. Marrying young. Struggling to make ends meet. Having her children so early." She turned on the water before continuing, "When Mom found out Dad had a mistress—"

"Whoa." Asa squeeze her eyes tight. Her arms hung at her side. She couldn't muster the strength to place them in her lap. "Mistress? What the hell are you saying, Dakota? Not our father. You can't be serious." Asa gasped for air. She willed her hands to stop trembling. "Who? What's her name?"

"We have no idea. It's not like Mom and Dad shared all that with us."

Ice dropped from the icemaker. The oven timer rang. Asa couldn't move. Her sister continued to stare at her as she took several deep breaths. The quiet that settled over the room was a relief. It allowed her to think. She remembered her mother's words "Honey, I just want so much more for you." Her mother told her that a dozen times.

"Are you upset with me for not telling you sooner?" asked Dakota.

"Hell, yeah. How could everyone keep that from me? What was the purpose?" Asa demanded.

"We weren't trying to keep it from you. It was just easier not to talk about it. This place already felt like a morgue, you were the only cheerful note around here." Dakota turned off the water and faced her sister.

Asa shook her head. "Simeon thinks his family was dysfunctional. It seems every family has a little dysfunction. At least he knew what he was working with." She placed her hands in her lap. "I guess I didn't make it easy for Mom to talk to me. I was always so defensive. Do you know how hard it is to admit it when your marriage is in trouble?"

"I think it's easier to walk across burning sands." A tear rolled down her sister's face.

This was supposed to be a happy night, a joyous occasion. But the revelations hardly qualified as celebration. The solid ground Asa expected to have at home seemed to be crumbling under her feet.

"Some celebration this turned out to be." Dakota leaned against the counter. "Well for sure, love affairs look different for the people in them." She dried her hands on the paper towel and faced her sister. "Now what? Everything is different. Who knows? Everything I thought was true just got turned upside down in one night." Asa pushed away from the table.

The oven timer rang again. Asa padded across the tile floor and pulled open the door. The edges of the pie bubbled, the sticky syrup streamed over the crust. "Who's ready for dessert?" She shoved the pie on the back of the stove and threw the potholder in the sink.

Concern dotted her sister's eyes. Asa waved her hand. "I'll be okay. Stop worrying. Did you check their room to look for any indication of what they planned to do?"

Dakota exchanged looks with her without replying. "Well, did you?" Asa asked again. "We boxed up a couple of their drawers—" Dakota stopped for a moment. "But we never checked those boxes in the bottom of the closet," Dakota finished.

Asa ran out of the kitchen. She scaled the stairs two at a time with the dog right behind her.

"What do you expect to find?" Dakota followed her up the steps.

"Something. Anything that will tell me what was going on." Asa turned the knob and stepped into her parents' bedroom.

With Dakota by her side, Asa dragged a box out of the

closet. She took a deep breath before peeling back the flaps. Together they pulled out old birthday and Father's Day cards, Asa's baby book, a few old report cards, and an assortment of pictures of their parents.

Asa sat back, resting on her heels. She ran her fingers through her curls as she looked around for something more.

"What did you expect to find?" Dakota asked.

"I don't know." She hunched her shoulders. "A journal, an appointment book with rendezvous dates or a business card from an attorney. Something."

"You're pretty good at this, huh?"

"I had a cheating husband."

"You know Mim and Pepe could have sanitized this room after the accident."

"Why would they do that?" Asa asked.

"To protect us."

§ § §

After her sister left, Asa stretched out on the living room sofa. The dog jumped up next to her and laid his head in her lap. Emptiness settled around her.

The house was quiet. The dog's fur felt soft against her hand. The fog she thought she left behind in Atlanta, clouded her thoughts. It was time for her to face the truth. After the secrets revealed tonight, she needed to examine the secrets she refused to face; her relationship with Simeon. She wanted a commitment; he wanted to focus on his business. Love had betrayed her before, she couldn't let that happen again. She couldn't waste another minute hoping for the impossible.

Scruffy lifted his head. His ears stood straight up, he charged off the sofa and barked at the door.

Asa didn't bother looking through the side panel. She opened the door for Simeon.

"I missed you." He gathered her in his arms and kissed her, devouring her tongue like a hungry man. She wrapped her arms around his waist. Her body pressed against him. God, she was going to miss him.

When he released her, she said, "I missed you too. It seems like we've been apart for weeks."

She led him into the living room. "Why the sad look? I thought you said your trip was good?" He pulled her into his lap.

She nuzzled under his chin to enjoy his warmth. "The trip was fine. It's family drama."

"Do you want to talk about it?" She laid her head on his shoulder. After a heavy sigh, she recounted the conversation that she had with her sister.

"Wow, that's heavy," he replied when she finished.

It's almost as if I've lived my whole life under false pretenses. I thought we were this happily ever after family and we've got secrets buried in our closet just like everyone else. I don't understand how I could have been so blind."

"Believe me, you were better off not knowing. Your

family cared enough about you to shield you from the ugly side. It didn't form the person you are today."

She pulled away from. "But it did. Instead of looking at life in a true way, I'm always looking for the bright side. The optimistic view, thinking all people are good and will do the right thing. But life doesn't always work that way. I know that now."

She placed her head back on his shoulder and ran her hand over his chest. His tight muscles felt like steel. He reclined and rested his head against the back of the couch. His breathing was slow and even. Her love for him curled around her heart, moistened her core, and made her tingle all over. Her body reacted this way whenever she thought about him. But her feelings weren't reciprocated. No other man had ever made her feel so helplessly giddy. But staying around until the fire in Simeon's eyes died out and he moved on to his next conquest would destroy her. Maybe what she wanted didn't exist, but she refused to settle or live another lie. Even her parents' marital happiness turned out to be a façade.

The sooner she accepted the truth, the sooner life could move forward. Her truth was tonight. Her longing for him would last a lifetime, but she'd find a way to manage. Just like she'd done when her parents died. She hoped Mim was right when she said, "Time heals all wounds."

His warm hands pushed her dress above her thighs. She spread her legs, allowing his hand to rest between her thighs. The warmth from his hand mushroomed through her core, across her breasts, and down her spine. She whimpered with pleasure. He kissed the hollow of her neck. She released his shirt from his pants and pressed her palm on his chest. The pulse of his heart echoed against her hand like a drum. Leaving him would be the hardest thing she ever did. But she couldn't allow her feelings for him to swallow her or push her down a dead-end road.

She found his mouth and wrapped her tongue around his. With her tongue she traced his lips then she pulled gently on his bottom lip. Her breathing came in short gasps that she couldn't control. She wanted to fill all her senses with his essence.

"Stand up," he whispered. His voice was so hoarse she barely heard him.

He lifted her off the couch and tugged her thong down her legs. He ran his hands along her legs under her dress, stopping long enough to knead the back of her thighs. His head was buried against her stomach.

"Where's the light?" his voice was husky. "Why?"

"I want to see you. I've been making love to you in my head since high school. I want to see everything from now on."

She turned on the table lamp without moving away from him.

He slipped his finger inside of her shooting off a shiver that flared across her body. She pushed the apprehension away and pulled her dress over her head and dropped it on the floor. The muscles in her legs tightened to keep her upright. Each kiss he planted down the length of her body heightened her desire. By the time his tongue found her core, she couldn't hold her hips still. Her body came alive with each thrust. Each stroke of his tongue sent a wave of ecstasy over her body. Nothing else mattered—not her job, not the house, not the uncertainty of tomorrow.

"I want you, Simeon." He laid her down on the couch and held her gaze while he peeled off his clothes. After removing a condom from his wallet and slipping it on, he entered her with such force she arched off the couch. He remained motionless for several moments with the thickness of his shaft throbbing inside of her. She wrapped her legs around his back, enticing him to pick up the tempo, but his thrust remained slow and controlled. He pushed deeper with each movement. She couldn't fight her feelings another moment. As the last wave of ecstasy washed through her, she cried out his name and held on to him. He stiffened as his lunges came faster. He threw his head back and in a strangled voice he called out her name before collapsing on top of her.

After years of yearning and wishing, she had what she wanted. But it wasn't hers to keep. This was the danger zone and she needed to get out while she still could.

§ § §

Simeon sat up in the bed. Asa's shallow breathing echoed in the room. No matter the outcome he had to tell her. He promised to be honest and he always kept his word. She felt so soft.

"Do you always wake up so early?" she asked

"I just want to spend as much time with you as I can. I enjoy you more when I'm awake." He chuckled. "You haven't asked me about the house. I expected you to pounce on me as soon as I walked in the door last night." Simeon ran his finger from her jaw along her golden shoulder.

"Yeah, after the conversation with Dakota yesterday, I'm not so sure I want to stay here. The house seems secondary." She hunched her shoulder. "It's like finding a treasure, the one you thought you couldn't live without only to open it and find it empty." There wasn't a twinkle in her eye. "So you have news?"

"The strip mall will be built on the west side, near Sellers Point."

"So Golden Leaf is going to be okay?" She pushed up on her elbow.

"Let me finish. The planned community with the center can't be built on the parcel of land that we planned. The only available parcel that works is Golden Leaf. We have to build it here. If we don't it could be years on the drawing board."

Asa fell back against the bed.

"There are hundreds of people that need that center. I hope you understand."

She stared at the ceiling without blinking.

"Aren't you going to say anything? Aren't you going to go ballistic and swat me?"

She was quiet for another minute. Tears gathered in the corners of her eyes.

"I know that's not what you wanted to hear. But we

don't have any other choices." His thumb swiped the tear away.

"It's okay. I understand," she said.

"We'll find you another place to live. A glorious house, even if I have to build it myself." He paused, adjusted his position. "One night I made a promise to my mother. I promised I'd build a place for low-income families to live. A place they could be proud to call home. When we started putting this project together, countless people told me how much the city needed this community center.

"You know, your news didn't knock me off balance as much as I thought it would. My sister's news already did that." She shook her head. Her curls covered her eyes. "It's okay. After last night...hearing about my parents' relationship, it made me realize it's not about the house." She looked around the room. "Maybe it never was. What I'm looking for is...it won't be found in an old five bedroom house."

Simeon brushed her hair away to see her eyes. He searched her face. "Then why are you crying?"

She sat up. The morning sun fell across her breasts. She placed her hands in her laps without looking at him. Something was different. The air in the room stood still. Even the dog was quiet at the foot of the bed.

"Simeon…" She paused. "I don't think this is going to work. You and I."

"Since when?" He sat up beside her in bed. "Is this about the house?"

She wrung her hands. "No. It's not the house. It's

everything else." She spread her arms, encompassing the room.

"What's everything?"

"If the house comes down, at least it won't be for something frivolous like a strip mall. Your planned community has something everyone can enjoy. I think Mim would have liked that. But a lot has happened in the last twenty-four hours. You know—" She turned her body toward him. "I came back to Bristol thinking I was going to put my life back together. Everything I knew about myself...everything I thought was true was here. But it's not. Once again the ground under my feet has begun to crumble. If I don't know anything else, I know I need to find my own truth. It won't be this house, it won't be our relationship." She folded her hands in her lap again.

He touched her chin, turning her head to look at him. "So what are you saying?"

Tears rolled freely down her cheeks. "Simeon, I love you. I told you weeks ago, even though you ignored me." She chuckled but didn't smile.

"I care about you, too. More than I've ever cared for anyone. It's just that right now—"

"I know. Your business comes first. You're busy. My head can understand that, it's my heart that's having the problem. I've been second fiddle in a relationship once before and once was enough for me. Maybe one day our paths will cross at just the right time. For both of us."

"But—" She placed her finger over his lips to silence him.

The only thing he could do was nod.

I just can let go. I can't expose myself to being hurt.

Chapter Twenty-Three

Asa stumbled over a box to grab the ringing phone.

"What are you doing?" Dakota inquired.

"Packing boxes." Asa stuffed newspaper into the box and taped down the flaps. "I thought you were coming over."

"I'll be there as soon as I can close up the bookstore."

"Don't worry about it. I didn't bring much from Atlanta. What little stuff I wanted from the house I packed up already. The rest can go down with the house. The truck will be here in a few hours to pick up the last of the boxes. Everything should be done by the time you arrive," Asa said.

"So, have you talked to him?" Dakota inquired.

"No. I think we've said everything there is to say. I've accepted it."

"You've accepted what...the house or the status of your relationship with Simeon?"

"Both." She sighed heavily. "It will be easier to get over the house than to get over Simeon. He's charming and gallant. I thought we had finally changed, had stopped doing that silly dance where I stepped forward and he stepped back. I even told him I loved him."

"You what?" Dakota yelled so loud Asa had to hold the phone away from her ear.

"I know, I know. I should have kept my mouth shut."

"Do you love him?"

"Yes, I love Simeon. I've loved him since high school. I probably loved him in grade school when he looked under my dress, too. But his work is his priority and I never want to be second in another relationship."

"What are you going to do now?"

"I'm a big girl, Dakota. I've been chasing that man for too long. He's got something to prove and I won't come between him and his mission. I don't want to wait around hoping he can conquer his demons. I'm done. One failed marriage teaches you a lot." She paused for a moment. "But, anyway, a community center with housing for senior citizens is something this neighborhood needs. I talked with Mrs. Donald before she left to visit her daughter. When the cottages are complete she's moving back here. She was so excited about not having to leave her church and her friends."

"So it seems like some people got the happy ending. But what about you? What are you going to do?" Dakota asked again.

"I'm going to do what I always do. I'm going to design something beautiful and expensive, then find somewhere really nice to wear it. There's the doorbell, hold on a second."

Asa ran down the stairs with Scruffy barking behind her. She pulled open the door. "May I help you?" she asked the stranger in the dark blue suit. "Are you Asa Conroy?"

"Yes, and you are?"

"Brad Stevens, from Harper Enterprise. I'm checking

with the neighbors of Golden Leaf to see if Harper Enterprise can assist with the packing."

"I think I have everything under control." She glanced at the stack of boxes behind her. "Did Simeon send you?"

"No. Not specifically."

She shifted her weight and turned away. "Thank you, Brad. I think I can handle everything."

Asa watched him cross the street and knock on another door. She half wished Simeon had been the one checking on her. She wanted to asked about Simeon, but living in the past was no fun. Two weeks wasn't enough time to stop her heart from racing every time she thought about him.

"Come on, Scruffy." She ushered the dog back into the house before closing the door.

"Who was it?" Dakota asked when she came back to the phone.

Asa relayed the conversation as she placed a wedding picture of her grandparents in a box and sealed it.

"I've cleaned out the spare room. Do you want to stay with me tonight?"

"No, I want to stay in the house for the final night. My new furniture is being delivered to the loft tomorrow, so I'll be fine."

"Suit yourself. I'll be there in a few hours." Dakota disconnect the call.

Asa turned out the light in her grandparents' bedroom and pulled the door closed. Her final sweep of the house found everything in order. The few boxes left would be loaded in her car tomorrow morning.

She touched the doorknob of her parents' bedroom. Maybe the sadness she saw in her mother's eyes during their last visit to Atlanta had nothing to do with her. Asa gripped the tarnished knob. The look that lurked behind her mother's eyes could have been tied to her own breaking heart.

"Be happy, Mom and Dad. I will," she whispered. She rubbed her hand over the closed door before retreating to her bedroom.

I'll keep the memories of the last few weeks tucked in my heart, forever.

Chapter Twenty-Four

Asa parked her car and jumped out with Scruffy right behind her. In the last five days a chain-link fence had been constructed around the community preventing her from parking any closer to what used to be home. The ground under her feet was saturated by the rain from last night. She removed her expensive sandals and placed them on the back seat of the car. Better to ruin her thirty-dollar pedicure than her four hundred dollar shoes.

Nothing about Excalibur Street looked familiar now. Mounds of dirt and asphalt dotted the landscape. The roar of heavy equipment assaulted her ears. Her palms were sweating. She swiped them against her shorts as she looked around the deserted area. Parked behind the fence she could see several cars and trucks; many of them boasted the name Harper Enterprise. She swallowed, expecting anger to clog her throat, but the anger didn't materialize. A good sign. She could move on, get on with her life.

With her fingers threaded through the links of the fence she squinted at what used to be her home. Where were the other residents? Didn't they want to witness the destruction as it unfolded? Scruffy whined and tugged at his leash to get behind the fence.

According to Dakota, the happy family tableau imprinted on her memory was distorted. Always had been. She kicked a dusty mound with her toe and watched the dirt settle back down. She had two options; hold on to her memories the way they were or listen to her sisters' version of the story. She had the balance of the summer to decide which version suited her best. She smirked, knowing reality would win. Her rose colored glasses were now buried in the same box with her divorce decree. Letting Simeon go was the hardest part. Maybe she would never stop loving him, but she had to keep moving forward.

She inched along the fence so that she could see the house from where she stood. Sweat dripped between her breasts, she pulled her blouse away from her abdomen and allowed the cool air to touch her skin. The heavy equipment went silent. In the distance, she could hear one of the workers yelling a greeting to his co-worker. She pulled her phone from her purse.

"Dakota are you coming down here?" she asked.

"No. The store is really busy this morning. Besides, I don't think that's a sight I want to see. Don't watch the demolition, Asa. Come down here with me, we'll get some ice cream. It will just make you sad."

"Believe it or not, I'm okay. I'm not as sad as I thought I would be. Knowing about Mom and Dad and how they felt about the house really changed my perspective. But I might take you up on that offer of food. Maybe we can even have a celebration of sorts. To my new life."

Asa heard her sister's heavy sigh. "Well, we don't know if Mom and Dad would have gotten a divorce. They may have decided to stay together and live happily ever after."

"Now who's living in La-La-Land?" Asa chided. "I'll call you later this evening. We can have dinner somewhere nice." Asa disconnected the call.

The huge yellow excavator roared to life again. It made a three quarter turn away from her neighbor's house to face her grandparents' house before coming to a stop. She could see the operator behind the wheel of the huge piece of equipment turning knobs. Maybe this was the moment when the phone was supposed to ring and the house would receive a stay of demolition.

The air was still as the machine idled. Several workers viewed a large blueprint while others tucked their hands in their pockets. After several minutes one worker rolled up the drawing and nodded at the operator behind the controls. The machine started again. The sway of the heavy metal ball increased in velocity. Slicing through the air without making a sound. It swung into the front of the house with a crash, crumbling it into a grotesque ugly snarl. Another swing of the ball brought the second floor of the house crashing down onto the first floor.

Asa couldn't turn away from the hideous sight. The ball made several more swipes at the house before it resembled the other piles of rubble. Half expecting tears, she reached into her purse, but instead of a tissue she opted for gum instead.

She couldn't find anything recognizable anymore as she looked back through the dust clouds at the pile of shingles, wood, and drywall. Even the magnolia tree that used to cover part of house lay on its side, its roots exposed.

"How quickly things change." She knelt down and rubbed Scruffy's chin. The dog lifted his head to give her more surfaces to scratch. "I believe everything happens for a reason. Just so I wouldn't be so lonely, you showed up on my doorstep, didn't you, sweetie."

With his rough tongue, he licked her cheek. "I love you too, puppy. Let's get outta here." She made her way along the fence without looking back. The scene behind her belonged in the past and it had to stay there. That included Simeon and what may have been.

"Well, Scruffy that was really quite liberating wasn't it?" They rounded the corner into the blinding sunlight. She used her free hand to shield her eyes. Her sunglasses were on the passenger seat of her car.

Even with the glare of the sun she recognized the tall, lean figure approaching. The swagger, the narrow waist, and long strides; she knew them in her sleep. Her heart thumped. It couldn't always be this way when she saw him. If she was going to stay in Bristol she had to find a way to see Simeon and not lose her composure. Her feeling for him was something else she had to let go of.

"I should have known I'd find you here," his deep baritone was barely audible over the sounds from the construction.

"I needed one last look. A few minutes later and I would have missed it." She continued to make her way to her car. Scruffy sniffed Simeon's pant leg. "This is going to be a nice community when it is all done. You should be very proud."

He reached for her arm, slowing her down. "After all these years you still don't know me, do you?"

The genuine sound of his voice made her stop. Her

eyes fell on his hand, where it touched her bare arm. "Simeon, it's okay about the house. Maybe it's a good thing the house is gone. Now I'm free to do whatever I want without being haunted by what used to be."

"I'm not talking about the house, Asa." He pulled her closer. Scruffy weaved his leash through Simeon's legs.

"Oh, no, Simeon. We are not doing this again. This thing--" She looked down at the dog. "This thing we do, I move forward, you pull back. I'm not doing that anymore."

"You see, that's where you're wrong. I've never pulled back."

She put her hand up to stop his speech.

"That's what we do. We disagree. We fight. And what for? We have never even been a couple and we fight all the time. We can't even agree on what happened a few weeks ago." She touched his face. Her hand trailed across his rough cheek and down to his chin. He hadn't shaved yet. His handsome features tugged at her heart. How could she get him out of her heart? If she had to walk away, she wanted to remember the heat she felt every time she came into contact with him.

"A few weeks ago you told me you loved me." There was a hint of sadness in his voice.

"Oh, you did hear me. I thought you had gone deaf."

He pulled her into his arms. His dark eyes blazed. His tongue flicked her lips before he parted them. He started slowly, so slowly. She wanted his tongue to fill her mouth and claim her. Instead of pulling away, like she'd promised she'd do, she pressed her body against his. He made a noise, a hushed growl, as his hand moved up her back and squeezed her tighter.

She pulled away scarcely able to breathe.

"I love you, too, Asa. I've loved you for more years than you know. Since the day I broke your CD player and--"

"Is this a joke? Are you trying to make me feel better about the house? Because if you are, it's okay. I'm okay. Really I--"

"It's not a joke. I've been trying to ignore my feelings for you for almost ten years. After the last two weeks—I can't do it anymore. I've picked up the phone almost a hundred times since you kicked me out of your house." He leaned closer and whispered in her ear. "I thought I could live without you, and I can. But...I don't want to, what would be the use?"

The expression on his face matched the passion in his voice. He was sincere. The leash slipped from her trembling hand. "I love you, Asa. I always have. I always will. You stole my heart in high school and you still have it."

"Oh Simeon."

He dropped down on one knee and held her hand. "Say you'll marry me. Say you'll be the mother of my babies. Say we'll grow old together."

"You're serious? she murmured, trying to catch her breath.

"I've never meant anything as much as I mean this.

I'm a better man with you than I could ever be without you. I want to make a life with you. A life worth living, not just existing. I want to spend the rest of my life making you as happy as you've made me since you came back."

"But what about your business, Harper Enterprise? No commitment. No time."

"Lies I've told myself. Lies I can't accept anymore. I want you. Say you'll marry me." His eyes pleaded.

"Yes, yes, yes," she gushed. "Yes, I'll marry you. I'll have your babies and most of all I'll grow old with you. I'll grow gray hair, arthritis, old with you."

"That's what I'm talkin' about." He stood up and held her tight.

"You're serious, right."

He laughed. "I am." He picked her up around the waist and swung her around. Instead of putting her down, he cradled her, picked up the dog leash and carried her down the block.

"Simeon, I can walk." She squirmed in her arms. He opened the door to his car and slid her into the front passenger seat, then allowed Scruffy to jump onto the back seat.

"What about my car?"

"I'll send someone for it later today."

"But...but my shoes?"

"I'll buy you new ones. You're not getting away from me ever again, Asa Conroy."

This is happening. He loves me?

Epilogue

Asa peeked around the panel at the large crowd gathering in The Art Institute of New York City. The hum of the throng of people grew louder every minute. She could barely hear the thump of the bass music playing in the background. She spotted Dakota and Melissa seated in the front row on the left side of the runway with their heads pressed together, whispering. Having her sisters present should have calmed her, but not today.

She backed away from the entrance to the large auditorium. Behind her throngs of make-up artists and tailors scurried from one model to the next making last minute adjustments. She ducked out of the way of a seamstress with a mouthful of stick pins to find Simeon.

He stood just beyond the flurry of activity with his arms crossed and his chin lifted just enough to make him look like an Adonis. After so many years of wanting him and eighteen months of marriage, her love had not diminished. He still made her pulse race. How he managed to stay calm with all the hustle and bustle amazed her. She needed a hunk of his tranquility to settle her jittery nerves.

"How's my handsome husband?"

"More importantly, how's my beautiful wife?" He wrapped his arm around her waist.

"I'm so nervous," she said to him over the buzz in the room.

"Breathe, Asa. The show is going to be fantastic. Look around, every ensemble looks stunning. The colors are amazing." He paused to smile at her. "The early reviews for your collection are all good. This is not your first Fashion Week appearance. You're no longer a neophyte and you're no one hit wonder."

Asa noticed a tall, thin model, with a sleek ponytail and smoky gray eyes wearing her favorite piece in the collection. The color blocked red and orange dress she wore bared her arms and stopped just above her knees. The crisscross bodice accentuated her lithe frame. Asa could not help feeling reassured by the sight and Simeon's words.

He pressed his lips against her temple and held her tight. She slipped her arms around his waist. No matter how many times he hugged her, it always felt like the first time.

"You're right, but this never gets old for me. And this show is so much bigger than the one I did last year. I'm so excited."

"You should be. You planned our wedding, redecorated the house, and introduced a line of sportswear all in a year. Next to you I must look like a tortoise, trying to keep up." He rubbed the small of her back.

"Stop it. You work hard, too. Look at the community center. Within months you'll be celebrating the grand opening."

"We will," he beamed. "Everything is going well now." She pressed up on her toes and kissed his mouth. His tongue connected with hers for a brief moment before he pulled away.

The look on his face grew serious and his eyes

darkened. "But you have to promise me you'll slow down." He placed his hand on her swollen stomach. "You've got to take care of my two favorite girls. Remember what the doctor said about the last trimester."

She placed her hand on top of his and squeezed. "I promise I will. When we get back home the only thing I plan to do is take care of my husband and finish the nursery. The baby's room will be easy. All I have to do is search the Internet for the pieces I want. Taking care of you requires a bit more," she teased.

"Okay, I'll try to keep my hands to myself," he lifted his hand from her back.

She grabbed his arm and put it back around her. Then she placed her palm against his cheek. Her heart swelled in her chest. The last year had passed in a blissful, dizzying blur. "How did I get so lucky?" she asked.

"We. We're both lucky."

She kissed him.

We're more than lucky. Much more.

Other Books By Jacki Kelly

THE SWEET ROAD SERIES
The Sweet Road To Love
The Sweet Road Back

DATING JUST GOT SERIOUS
Blind Date
One Date At A Time
Date Me
A Single Date
Speed Date
Dating Just Got Serious – Box Set
Done With Dating

WOMEN'S FICTION
Packed and Ready To Go
Going Backwards

ABOUT THE AUTHOR

Jacki Kelly has written dozens of short stories and several books. She lives in the North East with her husband and one loveable dog. She loves hearing from her readers so please contact her.

Connect with her online:
http://www.jackikelly.com
Twitter - @jackikellybooks
http://facebook.com/jackikellyauthor

If you enjoyed reading The Sweet Road Home please tell everyone you know. Please post a review for other readers on your favorite reading forum.

Trademarks Acknowledgment

The author acknowledges the trademark status and trademark owners of the following wordmarks mentioned in this work of fiction: Mercedes: Mercedes-Benz USA, LLC Rolex: Rolex SA iPhone: Apple Inc. Thomas Pink: Louis Vuitton Moet Hennessey Group Hugo Boss: Hugo Boss AG